PORTFOLIO
FASTER

The bestselling author Ankit Fadia is a 28-year-old tech junkie who loves tinkering with computers, gadgets and everything tech. He hosts a show called *Geek on the Loose* for PING Networks and has had a popular series on MTV called *What the Hack!*, where he gave tips, tricks and tweaks to get more out of technology and the Internet. Widely recognized as a computer security expert, he has delivered more than a thousand talks in twenty-five countries, received several awards and trained more than 20,000 people in India and China. He has studied at Stanford University and was chosen as a Global Shaper by the World Economic Forum. Ankit loves to travel and has visited over a hundred countries. For more information, please visit his website http://www.ankitfadia.com.

Praise for the Book

'In this easy-to-read book, Ankit shares simple tips, tricks and tweaks that make digital life faster and more productive. Try it out—doing is believing!'—**Gita Piramal, business historian and author of the bestseller *Business Maharajas***

'There are so many digital tools available to us via the web and mobile. However, often we are unable to maximize the utility and efficiency these tools can bring to our lives. Without a doubt, Ankit's book will help simplify the lives of many of us. This book will deliver a wow moment more than a few times!'—**Kunal Bahl, Founder, Snapdeal.com**

'The world that we are in today comes up with something new now and then, and we fail to know them all and deal appropriately. Ignorance sometimes embarrasses us and, at other times, we suffer being left behind. It is worth acknowledging this book of Ankit, *Faster*, will be a guiding light to the digital world, which is, in fact, the closest mate of this generation. I like it, and congratulate him, and also give my wishes to all the readers. May it add mileage in our endeavours, each day and for the better.'—**M.C. Mary Kom, Padma Bhushan, 2013; Bronze Medal Winner, Boxing, London Olympics 2012**

'The world-renowned ethical hacker Ankit Fadia has done it again. This book is a must - read for everyone—young and old, men and women—and will surely make you more tech-savvy. Written in an easy-to-read-and-understand style, I am confident this book will help every individual make more out of their digital lives. I have personally learnt and implemented a lot of new things about even the most routine acts like sending an email. Must say, my digital life rocks today. Thanks, Ankit.'—**Amit Burman, Vice Chairman, Dabur India Limited**

'We all live, at least, two lives today . . . one our real life and the other our digital life. Ankit Fadia makes our digital life simple through this amazing book and allows us to maximize the potential of living in our digital world. The tips and tricks mentioned in the book will allow users to be productive and safe and make the best of the digital world to enhance their own potential.'—**Shantanu Prakash, Chairman and MD, Educomp Solutions Limited**

'Like the title suggests, this book aims to make our digital life lot simpler and more comfortable. It's these tricks which make you from an amateur to a pro . . . grab the book now!'—**Vishal Gondal, Founder, Indiagames Limited and Angel Investor**

'Ankit shows many tricks and tips to get more out of the Internet and mobile phone, our constant companions in the hyper-networked world we live in.'—**V.R. Ferose, Senior Vice-President, Globalization Services, SAP AG**

'As we are getting dependent more and more on devices around us, Ankit has helped in uncluttering the overload and smartly improve our productivity—in a non-techie way. A great help in our daily lives!'—**Vikrampati Singhania, Deputy MD, JK Tyre & Industries Ltd.**

'Considering we live a large part of our lives online, and pay as much attention to our virtual avatars as our real ones, we don't spend too much time understanding how deep the depths of the Internet are. Ankit Fadia is a navigator above par of the cyber ocean and is the right guide for anyone who cares for their online reputation. What's more, he makes the web understandable and easier and faster so that we get much more out of our time spent online. We cannot deny that our lives will only become more virtual and Ankit's book *Faster: 100 Ways to Improve Your Digital Life* is like getting keys to the Ferrari that is the speeding web.'—**Devita R. Saraf, CEO, Vu Technologies**

'Ankit is one of a kind! His book finally allows PLU (people like us) to safely navigate the digital highway . . . and enjoy the journey! Can't wait for his next 100 tips!'—**Manish Chokhani, Managing Director and CEO, Axis Capital Limited**

'This is a book everyone will love and a must-read! Ankit is one of the smartest, most hard-working, most efficient and most fun-loving people I know, and he has been able to achieve tremendous success in a short span of time thanks to his love for technology and, importantly, how he leverages technology to get things done quickly. In just the first five minutes of reading the book, I had already learnt multiple ways to make my digital life faster and more fun! I am glad he is sharing these gems with all of us, and look forward to reading more of his books in the time to come.'—**Rohan Verma, Executive Director, MapmyIndia**

'Ankit combines his deep understanding of the digital space with his passion for helping people navigate technology. He has the uncanny ability to present complex ideas in simple ways that everyone can understand. His latest book *Faster* presents a comprehensive toolkit that will help readers significantly enhance their productivity. I am sure it is going to be a runaway success!'—**Kulin Lalbhai, Executive Director, Arvind Mills**

'This book is both extremely relevant and useful in today's digital age. Each chapter contains things that you have always wanted to do but didn't know how. Can't wait to try some of these tips out!'—**Varun Swarup, Paharpur Cooling Towers**

'The subject matter of the book is indeed interesting and young students, in particular, will be inspired and excited to read it. The simple topics chosen and explained well will be a source of great knowledge to every reader. It is not just how to get more out of technology, but how to apply it to our daily lives to make it faster, better and more efficient! In this book, Ankit provides some of these answers for people like me who use technology every day.'—**P.P. Chhabria, Chairman, Finolex Cables Limited**

FASTER

100 WAYS TO IMPROVE
YOUR DIGITAL LIFE

Ankit Fadia

PORTFOLIO
PENGUIN

PORTFOLIO

Published by the Penguin Group

Penguin Books India Pvt. Ltd, 11 Community Centre, Panchsheel Park, New Delhi 110 017, India

Penguin Group (USA) Inc., 375 Hudson Street, New York, New York 10014, USA

Penguin Group (Canada), 90 Eglinton Avenue East, Suite 700, Toronto, Ontario, M4P 2Y3, Canada (a division of Pearson Penguin Canada Inc.)

Penguin Books Ltd, 80 Strand, London WC2R 0RL, England

Penguin Ireland, 25 St Stephen's Green, Dublin 2, Ireland (a division of Penguin Books Ltd)

Penguin Group (Australia), 707 Collins Street, Melbourne, Victoria 3008, Australia (a division of Pearson Australia Group Pty Ltd)

Penguin Group (NZ), 67 Apollo Drive, Rosedale, Auckland 0632, New Zealand (a division of Pearson New Zealand Ltd)

Penguin Group (South Africa) (Pty) Ltd, Block D, Rosebank Office Park, 181 Jan Smuts Avenue, Parktown North, Johannesburg 2193, South Africa

Penguin Books Ltd, Registered Offices: 80 Strand, London WC2R 0RL, England

First published in Portfolio by Penguin Books India 2013

ISBN 9780143419709

Design by Tara Upadhyay
Printed at Thomson Press India Ltd, New Delhi

CONTENTS

LOOK AND FEEL

SECURITY

FUN STUFF!

FOREWORD

When Ankit Fadia told me that he could detail a hundred simple
ways in which I could substantially improve my digital life, I was
intrigued but sceptical. No one else had made such a proposition in
over twenty-five years of my rendezvous with the digital world.
I first met Ankit about ten years ago at an entrepreneurship
conference in India. He was still in his teens. Since then, I have
been following his progress quite closely as he figures out more and
more ways to make this world technology-efficient and digitally
secure. I find his attention to detail and knowledge about the nitty-
gritty of technology quite remarkable.

The importance of this book clearly reflects in its application in my
daily life. I have an iPhone with around a hundred features, but I

use less than ten of them, either because I haven't had the time to figure out the functionality of the others, or was not able to benefit much when I did try. It was the same for all my other phones—and I must have had more than a dozen since the time I got my first mobile phone in 1996. This book cuts across the clutter by clearly outlining each need which is solved, with the steps to solve it. And it does all this in extremely simple language such that the lack of technical capability of the reader does not impact the usefulness of the book in any way.

For instance, I receive several hundred emails every day. Many are spam mails that made it past my filters, and these I simply delete. I reply to some immediately, and then there are some mails each day that I think I will reply to later, but then forget. The senders do expect a reply. Learning how to schedule emails to be 'boomeranged' back to the top of my inbox at a later date and time has changed my response rate by a significant margin. Finding out easy ways to schedule replies later has led to a better utilization of my time when I do have more of it. I now use my flying time to draft not only professional but also personal messages like sending birthday wishes etc. to family and friends, which I schedule for sending at a later predefined date and time. And there are several nifty tips and tricks in this book that can help you manage your time better.

With this book, one can make more productive, secure, fun and beautiful every single day in one's digital life. It cuts across gadgets, platforms and tasks that users encounter on an everyday basis. Did you know that you can get the movie-theatre effect while watching YouTube videos or explore the night sky using your mobile phone? I did not. It's simply fascinating stuff!

Every page in this book is an enthusiastic celebration of technology's ability to make lives better. What makes it even more wonderful is the ease with which it includes the non-tech-savvy user, since today, no one can be said to be outside the realm of technology. Next time, if Ankit tells me that he can list a thousand ways to make my digital life better, I will probably just be intrigued but no more sceptical.

Sanjeev Bikhchandani
Founder and Executive Vice Chairman, Naukri.com

INTRODUCTION

I grew up in Delhi and, like most other Indian boys, my dream was to play cricket professionally. However, when I was ten years old, my parents gifted me a computer, and it changed the course of my life forever. The first time I used the computer, it made me incredibly happy. Since then, I have found everything related to technology, gadgets and the Internet really fascinating. The thrill of things constantly changing technology-wise, and how it impacts all aspects of life, can be addictive. I still remember spending the better part of my teenage years tinkering around with software and hardware, trying to get them to do more things than what was prescribed. They say that forbidden fruit always attracts—hacking is a field that blurs the boundaries of legality and illegality. The lure of the unknown and a lot of other fun possibilities were what attracted me to it. When I was fourteen years old, I wrote my first book—*An Unofficial Guide to Ethical Hacking*—which received a very good response in the market. This encouraged me to convert my hobby of computer hacking into a full-time profession.

My day job is to train, advise and consult individuals, companies and governments on how to be secure on the Internet. However, what gives me even more pleasure is when I get to tinker around with technology and tweak it to make it work cooler, faster and better. There are very few things that I find more exciting than being able to stretch the limits of technology. Due to the proliferation of social networks, smartphones and applications, I'm constantly asked questions outside the hacking space, where people are curious about how they could optimize their digital lives. A few years ago, I started my own show on MTV called *What the Hack!*

Every week, VJ Jose and I shared simple tips, tricks and tweaks which made everybody's technological lives easier, faster and better. The response to the show was fantastic and played a significant role in encouraging me to think about writing this book.

If you use technology on a daily basis but wish that there was a way to improve your interaction with it, without necessarily getting very technical or geeky, I think you will find this book quite useful. As the title suggests, this book contains 100 simple ways that will make your everyday digital life cooler, simpler, faster, stylish and more productive. Each chapter will give you practical tips, tricks, tweaks, apps and tools that will help you stretch the limits of technology, so that you can get more out of it—at work, at home and while you are on the move.

If you know how to use a mobile phone or surf the Internet, consider yourself 'qualified' enough to be able to understand, use and benefit from this book. The language is simple and there are plenty of screenshots. The book is divided into four main sections—Functionality, Look and Feel, Security and Fun Stuff—feel free to read them in any sequence, based on your own preferences and interests.

You will find that there is a slant towards the Apple and Google-based platforms. That is merely a reflection of the market reality today, where the iOS and Android platforms are dominating the mobile space.

Just like most of you, I love free stuff as well, and almost everything discussed in this book is available completely free of cost. The rest are available for a very nominal fee that is well worth the price.

I have not been financially compensated by any application developer for any of the apps, tools, software or techniques that have been featured in this book. All the things covered in this book are things that I have personally used, loved and found useful enough to share with all of you. Not only have I thoroughly tested everything discussed in this book under various conditions, situations and platforms, I have also made sure that everything can be used equally effectively in both Indian and global scenarios.

The best thing about technology is the fact that it is dynamic and constantly changing, with new stuff coming out all the time. Based on the developments in the technology world, I intend to keep updating this book on a regular basis with the latest tricks and tweaks. If there are things that have helped you improve your digital life, and you'd like to share them with the rest of the world, do feel free to send them in. Keep reading, keep tweaking and let's make our digital lives better, cooler and faster!

FUNC
TION
ALITY

1. HOW TO SEND A SECRET MESSAGE THAT WILL SELF-DESTRUCT IN THE RECIPIENT'S INBOX

 < 120 Seconds

Sometimes you need to share private information (password, credit card details or bank account information) with a family member, friend or colleague. It is possible to simply send the personal information via email or a chat message to the recipient. However, there is a risk that they might forget to delete the message and your private information may still remain in their inbox or computer. This means that a malicious user, who manages to illegally access the recipient's computer or account in the future, could potentially access your private information and misuse it. Wouldn't it be fantastic to be able to share your private message with the recipient via a self-destructing message which automatically gets deleted once it has been read?

Burn Note and the Burn Note logo are registered trademarks of Burn Note Inc., used with permission.

This is where a very useful website known as **Burn Note (www.burnnote.com)** comes into the picture. It allows a user to send a message to someone else in such a manner that the message will be automatically deleted immediately or after a predefined number of seconds after it has been read. This ensures that your message remains truly private and cannot be accessed by anyone after it has been conveyed to the intended recipient.

In this example, let us assume that a family member needs your credit card number for an urgent purchase and you wish to share in the form of a secure self-destructing message.

All you need to do is to simply start your browser and connect to **www.burnnote.com** and type the private message of your choice in the space provided.

Cancel	BURN NOTE	
	Step 1: Create a Note	
	Credit Card Number: 4444 5555 6666 0000	
Options		Next

Burn Note and the Burn Note logo are registered trademarks of Burn Note Inc., used with permission.

For added security, it is not only possible to prevent the recipient from being able to copy your private message, but also to put a password on the self-destructing message. This gives you double protection against unauthorized access to your private information. Moreover, **Burn Note** also allows you to specify the number of seconds after which the private message will automatically self-destruct.

Click on the **Options** button to access all the various options available to you while creating the private message.

Burn Note and the Burn Note logo are registered trademarks of Burn Note Inc., used with permission.

Once you are done writing the private message and selecting the various options related to it, click on the **Send** button. **Burn Note** will now create a URL or link to a special temporary web page where your private message will be stored.

Burn Note and the Burn Note logo are registered trademarks of Burn Note Inc., used with permission.

To share the message with your friend, you simply need to send this link to your friend via email, chat or mobile application.

When the recipient opens the link, they will be taken to the special temporary web page where your private message has been stored. However, they won't be allowed to view the private message without entering the password (if you chose to set one).

Burn Note and the Burn Note logo are registered trademarks of Burn Note Inc., used with permission.

Only once the correct password is entered will the recipient be allowed to view your private message (in this case, your credit card number). The best part is that the private message can be viewed only once and will be automatically deleted after the predefined number of seconds (in this case 180 seconds).

The recipient of your private message also has the option to reply to your message with another self-destructing **Burn Note** private message from right within your message.

Some other popular websites that allow you to send similar self-destructing messages are:

▶ **Privnote (www.privnote.com)**
▶ **One Share (www.oneshar.es)**

2. HOW TO SEND HUGE FILE ATTACHMENTS VIA EMAIL

 < 270 Seconds

Gmail has a 25 MB size limit while sending attachments. This isn't enough when one wants to send a large file (video, presentation, high-resolution ad campaign etc). Usually, such a size restriction forces people to split the file attachments into multiple emails or use third-party file transfer websites like Dropbox. Unfortunately, third-party file transfer websites come with their own share of problems—most of them are not free, have annoying advertisements and can have security issues.

Google Drive is your own hard drive on the Google Cloud. If you have a Gmail account, Google by default gives you 5 GB of free storage space on **Google Drive**. In case 5 GB is not enough, it is possible to buy even more storage space. Using **Google Drive**, you can not only back up all your important files in case of loss, but also transfer them to your friends or colleagues. **Google Drive** allows you to upload specific files or even complete folders from your computer. It can be accessed at **http://drive.google.com** and is one of the easiest and most secure methods of transferring files and folders on the Internet. Compared to third-party file-sharing websites, the advantage of **Google Drive** is that it is completely integrated with all other Google products, including Gmail, and does not require a separate sign-up.

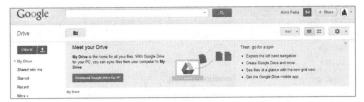

Google Drive and the Google Drive logo are registered trademarks of Google Inc., used with permission.

Google Drive and the Google Drive logo are registered trademarks of Google Inc., used with permission.

Once you log in to your **Google Drive**, you can immediately start uploading files or folders to your Google Cloud by clicking on the **Upload** button.

There is almost no limit on the number of files you can upload or the size of the files you can upload to your **Google Drive**, as long as you have space available in it.

You can monitor the status of an upload in the upload status window in the bottom right corner of the screen. You don't need to wait for a file to be completely uploaded before you start uploading another file. It is possible to simultaneously upload as many files as you wish.

Once a particular file or folder has been successfully uploaded to your **Google Drive**, you can click on the **Share** link to manage the sharing settings for that file. You can choose to keep the file private, public, or share it with specific people by simply clicking on the **Change** link under **Who Can Access**.

Google

Settings

General   Editing

Language:	English (United States) ▾
Time zone:	Choose a time zone.. ▾
Where items open:	⦿ In a new window ○ In the current window
Update indicators:	☑ Bold any updated items.
Storage:	**Using 1.8 GB of 31 GB (189 MB in Trash)** Only stored files (.PDF, .DOC, .JPG, etc.) count towards your storage limit. Get more storage

Google Drive and the Google Drive logo are registered trademarks of Google Inc., used with permission.

Google Drive and the Google Drive logo are registered trademarks of Google Inc., used with permission.

There are four different ways to share the file uploaded to your **Google Drive:**

1. Publish the file on the Internet, so that anyone with an Internet connection can access the file without any permission or authentication, just like a public blog or website

2. Keep the file completely private, so that only you can access it

3. Share it with specific Gmail accounts. This setting requires the recipient to sign into their Gmail account to verify their identity

4. Send a direct link (full URL) to the file to specific users. These users do not need to have a Gmail account

It is also possible for you to use **Google Drive** to control what people can do with the shared files. You can either allow them to only view your files, view and comment on them or even edit them.

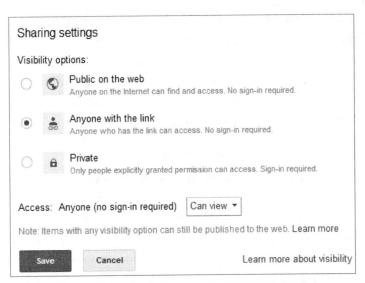

Google Drive and the Google Drive logo are registered trademarks of Google Inc., used with permission.

In other words, **Google Drive** is also very useful if you wish to collaborate with team members or friends and work together on the same files. In this example, I've chosen to share the uploaded file by sending a link to a specific set of people and would like to only assign viewing rights.

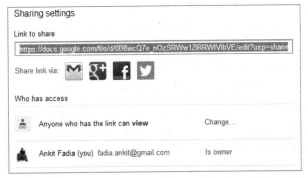

Google Drive and the Google Drive logo are registered trademarks of Google Inc., used with permission.

Google Drive will now create a direct link or URL which can be used to access the shared file. You can share this link or URL with friends or colleagues via email, chat or text message.

Even if you are using your work email account, you can still use **Google Drive** to transfer large files. Some other popular websites that allow you to easily transfer large files are:

▶   **Dropbox (https://www.dropbox.com)**
▶   **Sky Drive Live (https://skydrive.live.com)**

It is also possible to download mobile apps of **Google Drive**, Dropbox and Sky Drive to your Android or iOS device, so that you can easily share files from your mobile devices with your friends and colleagues.

3. HOW TO E-SIGN A DOCUMENT

 < 120 Seconds

There was a time when, each time you needed to sign an agreement and send it to a client, customer or partner, you would have to print out the agreement, sign all the pages and then courier the documents. However, in today's Internet age, many agreements can be executed digitally as well, by simply printing out the agreement, signing it, scanning it and then emailing it out. There is a faster and easier method of executing digital agreements—using online digital signing websites.

One of my favourite online e-signing websites is **DocuSign (http://www.docusign.com)**, which makes electronically signing and executing agreements extremely easy, fast and convenient. **DocuSign** allows users to sign any document with a single click of the mouse and send it out to the respective parties. Moreover, if you wish to request a signature from somebody, you can use **DocuSign** to send the document or agreement out for signing. Finally, **DocuSign** will also securely store all your digitally executed agreements on their cloud servers in one place for easy access in the future.

To start using **DocuSign**, you need to first create an account for yourself. Depending upon your needs, you can choose a relevant pricing plan. For home users, **DocuSign** is completely free.

Once you have created your account, you need to log in to be able to start digitally signing and sharing agreements and documents. The first time you log in to your **DocuSign** account, you will need to create a digital signature for yourself by clicking on the **Edit** button in the **DocuSign ID Card** box.

This will open up the **Manage Identity** page, which allows you to manage all the details related to your digital identity and digital signature for your **DocuSign** account. Now click on the **Manage Your Signature** link.

You can now create or manage the digital signature of your **DocuSign** account. You have the option to either upload a scanned copy of your digital signature (in the form of an image), draw your own signature using your mouse, or use one of the standard styles of signature on the **DocuSign** website. This page will allow you to set up not only your complete signature, but also a separate initials signature for your digital identity. Moreover, you can use this same page for setting up different digital signatures for different people in your organization or team. And, depending on the document that needs to be signed, the relevant person's digital signature can be applied to it using **DocuSign**.

Once you have set up the digital signature associated with your account, to sign a document that you have received, you simply need to click on the **Sign a Document Now** button in your **DocuSign** account. You can either upload the document that needs to be signed from your computer or from any of the popular online cloud services (like Google Drive, Sky Drive, DropBox and others). **DocuSign** supports most popular file formats, including but not limited to .doc, .pdf, .xls and .txt.

Once you have added the document that needs to be signed to your **DocuSign** account, simply click on the **Sign** button. **DocuSign** will now allow you to choose the type of signature you wish to put on the document (complete or initial), the portion of the document you wish to sign (drag and drop) and also size of the signature you want. Not only that, **DocuSign** also allows you to add other details of your digital identity (first name, last name, full name, date of signing, email address etc.) to any part of the document.

Finally, once the document has been signed, simply click on the **Finish** button and **DocuSign** will allow you to email the signed document to recipients of your choice. You can also choose to download the signed document as a PDF file or a ZIP file to your computer by clicking on the PDF icon at the top menu.

Some other popular digital signature websites that you could also use are:

▶   **Right Signature (https://rightsignature.com)**

▶   **Echo Sign (http://www.echosign.com)**

4. HOW TO STOP WASTING TIME ONLINE

 < 60 Seconds

Are you an expert procrastinator? Do you spend a lot of time in front of your computer aimlessly staring at the screen instead of studying or working? Are you addicted to Facebook and do you spend too much time stalking people you don't even know? Have you ever started watching videos online, lost track of time and then suddenly realized that several hours have passed? If these questions sound familiar, then welcome to the procrastinators' club that no one wants to be in, yet has millions of members. Research reveals that taking short breaks from work helps you remain more focused and efficient. However, for most of us, a short break invariably turns into a long sabbatical from work. Here, we are going to discuss strategies and tools that will help you win the time battle against that technological black hole called the Internet.

It is impractical to completely stop using popular websites like Facebook, Twitter, Sports Portals, YouTube, and gaming and other sites. However, wouldn't it be great if there was a way to restrict the amount of time per day you are allowed to spend on each of these websites? There is a very popular Google Chrome browser extension called **StayFocusd** that helps you with just that. You can download it free of cost from the Google Chrome Web Store **(http://bit.ly/ricj4s)**.

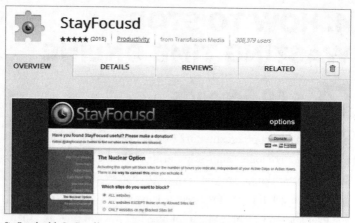

StayFocusd and the StayFocusd logo are registered trademarks of Transfusion Media, used with permission.

Once you have installed **StayFocusd**, there will be a new icon or button that will be added to the URL bar in Google Chrome. Clicking on this icon will allow you complete control over the amount of time you can spend on each website every day. Once you exceed the allotted daily time of a specific website, it will no longer allow you to access it until the next day!

StayFocusd and the StayFocusd logo are registered trademarks of Transfusion Media, used with permission.

This is how you can use the **StayFocusd** browser extension to manage the amount of time you are allowed to spend on Facebook:

StayFocusd and the StayFocusd logo are registered trademarks of Transfusion Media, used with permission.

Open your browser to the Facebook homepage and click on the **StayFocusd** button in your browser. This will open the **StayFocusd** settings page for Facebook.

If you wish to restrict access to Facebook, click on the **Block this entire site** link or you can click on **Advanced options** to enter custom URLs to block only specific pages within Facebook.

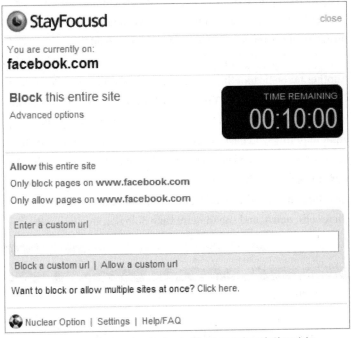

StayFocusd and the StayFocusd logo are registered trademarks of Transfusion Media, used with permission.

Once you have enabled restricted access to websites, click on the **Settings** link to specify the amount of time per day you are allowed to spend on all the restricted websites put together. If you want to completely block access to a particular website, then you set the number of minutes to 0. It is important to note that this time restriction is not website-specific but applies to all the blocked websites.

StayFocusd and the StayFocusd logo are registered trademarks of Transfusion Media, used with permission.

Not only is this tool very useful to restrict access to certain websites, but it also works for parents who are worried about their kids accessing adult websites on the Internet and want to block access to them. **StayFocusd** works only on the Google Chrome browser, but there are similar extensions/add-ons available on other popular browsers like Firefox and Internet Explorer as well.

Another fantastic tool that keeps you focused online is a Google Chrome extension called **Title Time Tracker**. You can download it from **http://bit.ly/nKAfvE**. Once installed, it displays the amount of time you have spent on a specific website in the title bar of the page. This sends you on a virtual guilt trip. The idea behind this application is that when you see the amount of time you are spending on these various websites, you will be able to exercise some self-control and spend more time doing productive work.

Google and the Google logo are the registered trademarks of Google Inc., used with permission.

If the Internet is not the only place you tend to waste time and you are also prone to wasting a lot of time doing non-work-related stuff on your computer, then I would recommend using a very useful application called **RescueTime (http://www.rescuetime.com)**. It is a very useful app that allows you to improve your efficiency by analysing all your activities on the computer. It tracks everything that you do on your computer, including the amount of time you spend on various websites and applications, working on documents, playing games, listening to music and just about everything else!

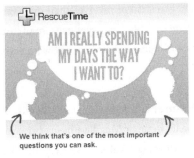

We think that's one of the most important questions you can ask.

RescueTime and the RescueTime logo are registered trademarks of RescueTime Inc., used with permission.

Hopefully these tools will enable to you achieve more per day or help you to get out of office earlier than usual.

5. HOW TO SEND AN EMAIL IN THE FUTURE

 < 270 Seconds

Think of these two situations: you are free right now, but don't need to send an email until a few hours later; or you need to send out a birthday greeting after four days, but work catches up and you forget to do it. Wouldn't it be wonderful if you could send out the email right now and forget about it, but the recipient receives it on his or her birthday? Or imagine that you are in a profession that requires regular updates or follow-ups on a periodic basis and wish to schedule all of it in advance. This is where **Boomerang for Gmail** is such a handy tool.

Boomerang for Gmail (http://www.boomeranggmail.com/) is a Firefox and Chrome plugin that allows you to take complete control over when you send or receive email messages in your Gmail account. Once enabled, you can use Gmail just the way you normally do, but with more control over how and when you send your emails.

To enable the **Boomerang** feature in your Gmail account, just open your Google Chrome or Mozilla Firefox browser (it does not currently work on Internet Explorer) and visit the **Boomerang** website. Click on the Install **Boomerang** button and simply follow the instructions that you see on your screen.

Once you have completed the installation process, the next time you log in to your Gmail account, the **Boomerang** feature would be enabled. **Boomerang** is very intuitive in its design and is extremely easy to use.

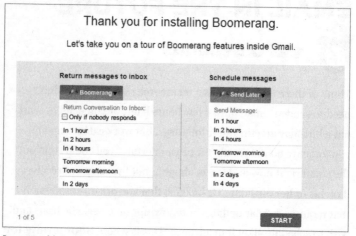

Boomerang and the Boomerang logo are registered trademarks of Baydin Inc., used with permission.

You can proceed to compose an email just the way you normally would. However, just below the Send button you will see the **Send Later** button that can be used to **Boomerang** the email and send it at a predefined later date and time. **Boomerang** allows you a range of time and date options to choose from—you could delay the email by anywhere between an hour to a few months. You could also choose a specific time and date in the future.

One of the **Boomerang** options that I use quite often is to schedule a recurring message to be sent to someone on a periodic basis. This feature is especially useful in case you need to follow up with a team member or a client about the same thing multiple times at periodic intervals. You can do this by simply clicking on the **Schedule Recurring Message** option

Boomerang and the Boomerang logo are registered trademarks of Baydin Inc., used with permission.

after clicking on the **Send Later** button.

Another situation where **Boomerang** plays a very useful role is when you receive an email that you do not want to deal with at that particular moment, but would like to be reminded of at a later stage. Or sometimes an email is sent to your entire team and you feel someone else in the team is more qualified to reply to it, but you want to be reminded about the email in case no one replies to it.

Whenever you open an email, on the top right corner you will see a **Boomerang** button. If you click on it, you will be able to schedule the email to be **Boomeranged** back to the top of your inbox at a future date and time. You can also configure it such a way that the email will be **Boomeranged** back to the inbox only if nobody responds to the email.

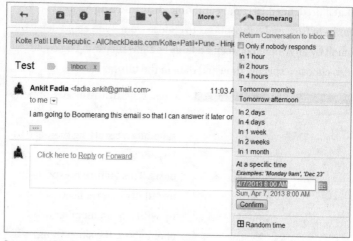

Boomerang and the Boomerang logo are registered trademarks of Baydin Inc., used with permission.

The same option to **Boomerang** an email to the top of your inbox at a future date and time is also available when you are composing a new email using your Gmail account. Simply enable the **Boomerang This Message** option and select when in the future you want the email to be **Boomeranged** back to the top of your inbox. As simple as that!

If you want to use **Boomerang** with your other email accounts (like Yahoo, Hotmail or your work email) and send emails in the future, it is possible to get **Boomerang for Microsoft Outlook**. However, unfortunately **Boomerang for Microsoft Outlook** is not free and costs $29.95 as a one-time fee.

6. HOW TO UNSEND AN EMAIL FROM GMAIL

 < 60 Seconds

All of us have experienced email regret, the state of mind that immediately follows:

1. An impulsive and emotionally charged email
2. An email accidentally sent without actually finishing it
3. An email with many typos and grammatical mistakes
4. An email with which you have forgotten to include a file attachment
5. A very personal email or a sensitive work email sent to the wrong colleague

In such situations, wouldn't it be great if it were possible to unsend an email even after it has been sent? This is where the **Gmail Undo Send** feature helps. Once enabled, the **Undo Send** feature allows you to unsend an email even after it has been sent. Think of it as Gmail's way of giving you a window of opportunity to fix your email sins of the recent past.

Once you enable the **Gmail Undo Send** option, every time you send an email, Gmail will not send it instantly, as is the normal practice. Instead, it will hold back the email on its server for a few seconds, allowing you to change your mind, retrieve and modify the email if you wish. This window of a few seconds to unsend emails can be a big life saver. To enable the **Undo Send** option in Gmail, all you need to do is follow the following steps:

Once you are logged in to your Gmail account, look for the **Settings** button on the top right corner of the screen in your inbox and click on it. The **Settings** button allows you to change all the various options and features related to your Gmail account.

Gmail and the Gmail logo are registered trademarks of Google Inc., used with permission.

Once you click on the **Settings** button, a drop-down menu list will pop up on the screen. Within the drop-down menu list, once again click on the **Settings** option.

Now click on the **Labs** tab to browse through all the **Google Labs** features available in your Gmail account. **Google Labs** basically contains experimental features that may still be under development. **Undo Send** is one of the features available as part of **Google Labs** in Gmail.

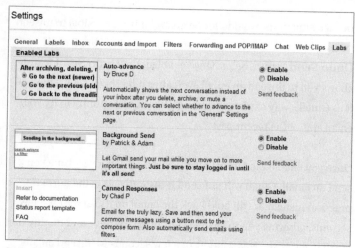

Gmail and the Gmail logo are registered trademarks of Google Inc., used with permission.

Scroll down the **Labs** page and look for the **Undo Send** option and enable it. Now all the emails that you send will be temporarily saved for a few seconds and will not be immediately sent. Once you enable

this option, make sure you scroll all the way down to the bottom of the
Labs page and save the changes.

Gmail and the Gmail logo are registered trademarks of Google Inc., used with permission.

Now that the **Undo Send** option has been enabled, let us try it.
Assume that it is your birthday and you are stuck in the office later
than usual, since your boss gave you a last-minute project to finish
within a ridiculous deadline. You are really frustrated with your
boss and impulsively type an email expressing your displeasure.
Although you intend to send this email to your friend, you are in a
hurry and you accidentally send the email to your boss!

Worst Boss Ever!

Ankit Fadia

Worst Boss Ever!

I am tired of working at this place. Cant wait to get out of here.

--
Warm Regards,

Ankit Fadia

http://www.ankitfadia.com

Facebook: http://www.facebook.com/ankitfadiaofficialpage
Twitter: http://twitter.com/ankit_fadia
MTV What the Hack: http://www.facebook.com/MTVWhatTheHack

Learn how to Unlock Everything on the Internet (websites, chat, torrents, download limits and just about every
than 20,000+ copies sold. For more details & to get your own copy visit: http://goo.gl/3wUpJ

Gmail and the Gmail logo are registered trademarks of Google Inc., used with permission.

The moment you send the email, you realize what has happened.
Under normal circumstances, once an email has been sent, there
is nothing that can be done. Fortunately, you have enabled **Undo
Send** and it allows you to change your mind about sending an email

even after a few seconds of clicking the send button. Once you send an email, you will see the following message displayed on the screen. If you click on the **Undo** link in the message within the next few seconds, you will be able to prevent the email from being sent.

Your message has been sent. <u>Undo</u> <u>View message</u>

Gmail and the Gmail logo are registered trademarks of Google Inc., used with permission.

As soon as you click on the **Undo** link, the email will be retrieved and will not get sent. You will see the following message displayed on the screen when the email has been successfully unsent:

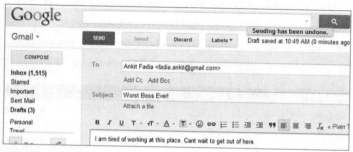

Gmail and the Gmail logo are registered trademarks of Google Inc., used with permission.

Gmail and the Gmail logo are registered trademarks of Google Inc., used with permission.

It is possible to control the number of seconds for which the **Undo Send** option is available after sending an email. Click on **Settings > General > Undo Send > Send cancellation period** and select the number of seconds that you wish to configure on your account. You can choose between 5, 10, 20 or 30 seconds.

If you want to unsend an email while using some other email account (Yahoo, Hotmail or your work email account), then you can configure the Microsoft Outlook email client to delay any emails you send by a few minutes.

7. HOW TO REMOTELY ACCESS YOUR COMPUTER FROM MOBILE DEVICES

 < 300 Seconds

Have you ever wished there was a way to remotely access the photographs, music, videos and files that are on your home computer from your mobile device while you are on the move? Would you like to access your files and documents while you are travelling? Want to show some pictures to your family or friends, but realize that the photos are not on your mobile phone, but on your home computer? Never be away from your data again—create your own personal cloud with the free app called **Polkast**.

Any files on your computer you choose to share via **Polkast** can be remotely accessed from any mobile phone or tablet you own. Unlike traditional cloud services, in the case of **Polkast**, all your files continue to remain on your computer, but can still be accessed remotely. No more worrying about carrying your pictures, videos, music and files everywhere you go!

For **Polkast** to work properly, you need to install the **Polkast** server app on your computer (from which you want to remotely access data) and the **Polkast** client app on your mobile phone or tablet. Both the server and client versions of **Polkast** are available as a free download from **www.polkast.com**. The **Polkast** app currently supports both Android and iOS platforms.

To get things started, you need to install the **Polkast** server app on your computer and register an account for yourself.

Polkast and the Polkast logo are registered trademarks of Polkast LLC, used with permission.

Next you need to choose which folders on your computer you want to make remotely accessible via **Polkast**.

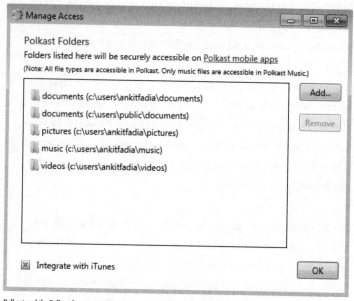

Polkast and the Polkast logo are registered trademarks of Polkast LLC, used with permission.

Once you start **Polkast** on your mobile phone or tablet, it will ask you to log in to your **Polkast** account.

After you are logged in, **Polkast** will automatically search for your personal cloud (your home-base computer) and connect you to it.

Polkast and the Polkast logo are registered trademarks of Polkast LLC, used with permission.

Once the **Polkast** app on your phone successfully connects to your home-base computer, the app dashboard will be displayed on the screen. The dashboard allows you to remotely browse, search, download and stream files from your home-base computer.

Polkast and the Polkast logo are registered trademarks of Polkast LLC, used with permission.

Tapping on the **Pictures** icon on your dashboard will allow you to browse all the photos stored in shared folders on your home-base computer. It doesn't matter where you are, as long as you have Internet access to connect to your personal **Polkast** cloud. You can share the photos on your favourite social network websites, edit them and even save them back to your personal cloud.

Tapping on the **Music** icon on your dashboard will allow you to remotely browse your favourite songs and playlists stored on your home-base computer while you are on the move with your tablet or mobile phone in hand. Why carry all your favourite music with you everywhere, when you can easily remotely stream it from your **Polkast** cloud to your mobile devices?

Polkast and the Polkast logo are registered trademarks of Polkast LLC, used with permission.

With the help of **Polkast,** you can create your very own personal cloud and remotely access all your material through your mobile phones and tablets from anywhere!

8. HOW TO MANAGE YOUR CONTACTS SMARTLY

< 120 Seconds

Have you ever lost touch with a business contact or a friend because the contact information you had saved in the address book of your mobile phone became outdated? Managing the contacts on your phone—so that you have everyone's latest contact information—and making sure that they have your most updated contact information can be tricky. But with the **Phonedeck** app on your mobile phone, managing your contacts and interacting with them will become a breeze.

Phonedeck is currently available as a free download for both Android and iOS platforms. Once installed on your phone, **Phonedeck** brings your contacts list to life by allowing your friends to remotely update their contact information (like phone numbers, email addresses, pictures) directly on your phone without your intervention. Similarly, it allows you to remotely update your contact information directly on your friends' phones. No more manually editing your contacts or losing touch with them if either your or their contact information changes! As long as both you and your contacts have **Phonedeck** on your respective phones, you will always be in touch.

Moreover, the **Phonedeck** app gives you a lot of interesting statistics about your phone calls and text messaging communication with your contacts. **Phonedeck** tells you the total number of phone calls and text-message interactions you have had with all your contacts in the past month. It also shows you your top contacts, how often you have communicated with them and the last time you communicated with them. Think of **Phonedeck** as an entire log of your phone and messaging habits and activities. Based on the communication habits shown by **Phonedeck**, you can opt for the most cost-effective mobile phone plan that suits you.

Since **Phonedeck** keeps a log of all your phone call and text messaging communication habits with your contacts, it can analyse your mobile phone activity, predict who you want to communicate with and display your most important and relevant contacts in the dashboard.

Another fantastic feature of the **Phonedeck** app is the fact that it allows you to remotely access all the contacts on your phone, so that you can send SMS text messages and initiate calls to them by simply logging in to **www.phonedeck.com**.

9. HOW TO IDENTIFY A CALLER WHO IS NOT ON YOUR CONTACTS LIST

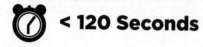 **< 120 Seconds**

Have you ever received a call from a number that is not stored in your contacts list and you wished there was a way to find out who is calling? Never get stuck talking to a boring relative you don't want to speak to—install the **True Caller** app on your mobile phone.

True Caller (http://www.truecaller.com) is a free app that can be installed on almost all mobile phone models, including phones that do not have a smartphone operating system. **True Caller** is a global directory containing millions of phone numbers that have been sourced from public directories, yellow pages and crowd sourcing techniques.

True Caller and the True Caller logo are registered trademarks of True Software Scandinavia AB, used with permission.

Once **True Caller** has been installed on your mobile phone, whenever you receive a phone call from a number that does not exist in your address book, **True Caller** will automatically attempt to identify the name of the unknown caller by searching for it in its global database. In other words, **True Caller** works like a caller ID for even those numbers that are not listed in your address book. In the example here, I receive a phone call from an unknown number on my Android phone and **True Caller** is able to identify the name of the caller almost instantaneously. The only thing **True Caller** requires for it to work is Internet access on your phone.

True Caller also allows you to type the name of a person and search for their number if it exists in any of the **True Caller** databases.

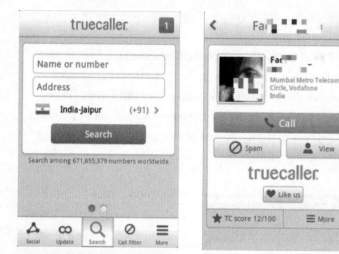

True Caller and the True Caller logo are registered trademarks of True Software Scandinavia AB, used with permission.

One of the techniques used by **True Caller** to grow its vast database of numbers is to opt in crowdsourcing. In other words, whenever someone installs the app on their phone, they have the option to enable something known as **Enhanced Search**, which will allow **True Caller** to upload all entries from that mobile phone's address book to their global database. By installing **True Caller**, your entire address book becomes a part of the publicly searchable **True Caller** database, without the permission of the people who own those numbers.

True Caller is obviously a very powerful tool. However, if you want to protect your privacy and want to unlist your phone number from their publicly searchable database, you can do it from **http://www.truecaller.com/unlist**.

10. HOW TO AUTOMATICALLY SHARE YOUR LOCATION WITH YOUR FRIENDS

 < 270 Seconds

Have you ever been late for a meeting and wished there was a way for you to share your location with your colleagues? Do you wish there was a way to share your location with your loved ones while travelling alone at night? Do you want to be able to track where your kids are when they are out late at night? **Glympse** can be used in these situations.

Glympse and the Glympse logo are registered trademarks of Glympse Inc., used with permission.

Glympse is available as a free download from **http://www.glympse.com** and works on most smartphone platforms like Android, iOS, Windows and BlackBerry. Once it is installed on your mobile phone, it can be used to easily share your current physical location on a geographical map with someone else for a predefined amount of time. The best part is that your location on the map that your friends can see will not be static and will automatically change dynamically with time as you move.

Install **Glympse** on your mobile phone and create your profile by adding your name and photo to the app, so that your friends know who you are. You can click on the **View Map** button to view your current location on a geographical map as denoted by a blue dot. **Glympse** uses the GPS feature on your phone to dynamically change your location.

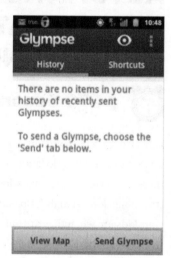

Glympse and the Glympse logo are registered trademarks of Glympse Inc., used with permission.

It is also possible to view your location on the map with a satellite view and get different details about your location (speed, altitude etc.).

To share your location with someone else, simply click on the **Send Glympse** button on the home screen of the **Glympse** app. It will allow you to share your location with your friends via various communication mediums like text message, email, Facebook, Twitter or even messengers like WhatsApp. Moreover, you can specify for how long your friends will be allowed to view your location. Not only that, you can even enclose a private message for your friends along with your current location. In the following example, I am going to share my location and a private message ('Almost there!') with my friend Ankit Fadia via a text message and I want to share my location for the next fifteen minutes.

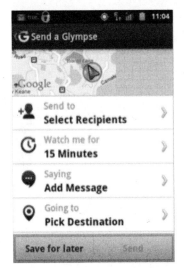 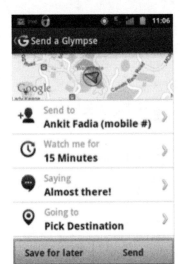

Glympse and the Glympse logo are registered trademarks of Glympse Inc., used with permission.

Within a few seconds, my friend will receive a text message containing my private message and a link to a web page that will display my geographical location. He does not need to have the **Glympse** app installed to be able to see my location. The link can be clicked from any computer or mobile phone, and it will show my

> **Here's my location, courtesy of Glympse -** http://glympse. com/Y69-2G7
>
> *Glympse and the Glympse logo are registered trademarks of Glympse Inc., used with permission.*

location, which will be updated constantly. The live updates of your location can be very useful for your friends to keep a track of how far you are from your destination. **Glympse** also displays how fast the user is moving, so that my friend can estimate how much time it will take for me to reach my destination.

Glympse also allows you to enter your destination address when you are sharing your location with your friends. This can be very useful in estimating the amount of time it will take you to reach the destination.

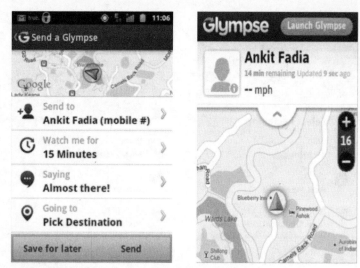

Glympse and the Glympse logo are registered trademarks of Glympse Inc., used with permission.

Once the predefined time period passes, then my friend will no longer be able to view my current location and only the last updated location will be shown to him.

11. HOW TO SEARCH YOUR GMAIL ACCOUNT LIKE A PRO

 **< 60 Seconds**

If you are a heavy email user, finding an email that you may have sent or received several months ago can be quite a tough task. **Gmail** makes it very easy for users to find emails that match certain parameters and filters right from the search box at the top of your **Gmail** account page.

Google and the Google logo are registered trademarks of Google Inc., used with permission.

Using the **from:** search operator, you can search for an email sent to you from a particular email address.

Using the **OR** search operator, you can search for an email sent to you from a particular email address or from some other email address.

john@john.com OR peter@peter.com

Google and the Google logo are registered trademarks of Google Inc., used with permission.

Using the **to:** search operator, you can search for emails sent to a particular email address. For emails with a particular subject, use the **subject:** search operator. We are going to search for all emails sent to john@john.com with 'meeting' as the subject.

to:john@john.com subject:meeting

You can modify the previous example slightly and make the search even more powerful. Let us assume that you want to search for emails with a specific word in the subject ('meeting' in this case) and a specific word in the body ('Singapore' in this case).

to:john@john.com subject:meeting Singapore

It is also possible to search for only those emails that have an attachment using the **has:attachment** search operator. The next example will search for only those emails that have been sent by john@john.com, have the word 'meeting' in the subject and have a file attachment.

from:john@john.com subject:Meeting has:attachment

The **has:attachment** search operator also allows you to search for keywords inside actual file attachments.

has:attachment finance

If you wish to search for emails with a specific file attachment, **Gmail** also allows you to search with a specific file attachment name using the **filename:** search operator.

from:john@john.com filename:resume

If you wish to clean your inbox and increase the space available in it, it is a good idea to start by deleting emails with large email attachments. It is possible to search for all emails in your account with file attachments larger or smaller than a particular size. This can be done using the **smaller:** and **larger:** search operators.

from:john@john.com larger:15MB

from:john@john.com smaller:15MB

Using the **before:** and **after:** search operators it is possible for you to search for emails from a particular date or dates. To search for all emails sent from john@john.com on 14 November 2012, you can use the following search command:

from:john@john.com after:2012/11/14 before:2012/11/15

Another way to find emails from a particular date is by using the **newer_than:** and **older_than:** search operators. If you want to find all emails sent from john@john.com in the last two days, then you can use the following search command:

from:john@john.com newer_than:2d

While searching for a particular email, you can also specify where in your email account **Gmail** should look for it. This can be done using the **in:** search operator. The most popular uses of the **in:** search operator includes the following:

in:inbox
in:trash
in:spam
in:anywhere

from:john@john.com in:trash

If you wish to search for a keyword from a chat conversation that you had with a friend in **Google Chat**, then you need to make use of the **is:chats** search operator. If you want to search for the keywords 'nimesh' and 'cell' in all your **Google Chat** history, then you need to type:

is:chats nimesh cell

It is also possible to click on the down arrow button on the right side of the search box in your **Gmail** account to reveal advance search filters and options that you make use of for finding stuff in your account.

Search   ✕

Chats ⬍

From

To

Subject

Has the words

nimesh cell

Doesn't have

☑ Has attachment

Date within   1 day ⬍   of

Examples: Friday, today, Mar 26, 3/26/04

🔍   Create filter with this search »

Google and the Google logo are registered trademarks of Google Inc., used with permission.

12. HOW TO MANAGE ALL YOUR TO-DO LISTS

 **< 120 Seconds**

Do you like making to-do lists when you start your day? Do you have trouble creating, managing and sharing these to-do lists with your friends and colleagues? **Any.do (http://www.any.do)** is a free to-do-list management app that can be installed on your Android or iOS device and even in your Google Chrome browser as an extension. It saves all your to-do lists on the cloud and allows you to create, access and manage them on the move from anywhere. The best thing about the **Any.do** app is its sleek and easy-to-use interface that makes creating to-do lists extremely intuitive and fun.

Start your browser and connect to **http://www.any.do** to install the **Any.do** app in your Google Chrome browser or any of your Android or iOS devices.

Click on the **Register** link to create your account on **Any.do**, so that your lists can be saved on the cloud and automatically synced across all your devices. You also have the option to link **Any.do** with your Facebook account, if you want to avoid creating a separate account.

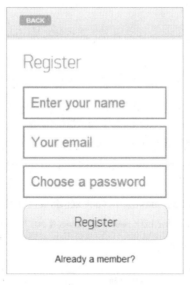

Any.do and the Any.do logo are registered trademarks of Any.do Inc., used with permission.

Once you have registered, you can start creating to-do lists and goals for yourself using **Any.do**. You can sort your to-do lists based on the date or category (**Personal**, **Work**, **Financial** and others). You can drag and drop tasks between categories or dates as you wish.

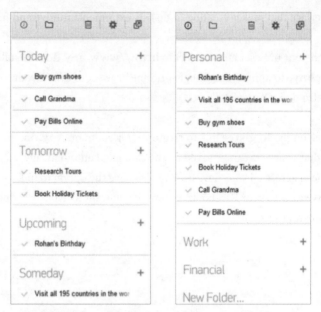

Any.do and the Any.do logo are registered trademarks of Any.do Inc., used with permission.

You can choose to mark particular tasks as priority, so that you know they are more urgent and important than other tasks on your list. You can add comments or notes to tasks, so that you can read them while performing the task. Most importantly, you can also assign reminders to your tasks, so that **Any.do** will remind you about them and help make sure they get done. Finally, once you are done with a particular task, you can cross it out by simply running your finger across it.

Any.do and the Any.do logo are registered trademarks of Any.do Inc., used with permission.

You can mark a task as a priority.

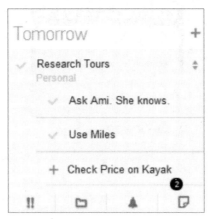

Any.do and the Any.do logo are registered trademarks of Any.do Inc., used with permission.

You can add notes to a task.

Any.do and the Any.do logo are registered trademarks of Any.do Inc., used with permission.

You can set reminders for tasks.

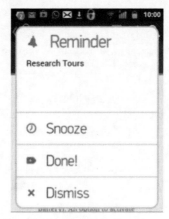

Any.do and the Any.do logo are registered trademarks of Any.do Inc., used with permission.

Any.do will remind you about tasks to make sure you do them.

Any.do and the Any.do logo are registered trademarks of Any.do Inc., used with permission.

Once you are done with a task, you can simply strike it off.

Once you have created a task, you can even share it with friends in your contact list, but this feature only works when you are using the **Any.do** app on your phone and will not work in the web version.

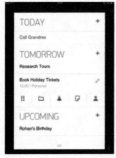 

Any.do and the Any.do logo are registered trademarks of Any.do Inc., used with permission.

My favourite feature of the **Any.do** app is the fact that if you install the browser extension in your Google Chrome browser, **Any.do** becomes completely integrated with Gmail. It will then allow you to add tasks and reminders to your **Any.do** app by clicking on the **Remind Me** button from right within your Gmail account.

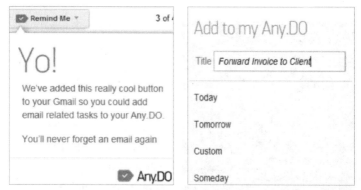

Any.do and the Any.do logo are registered trademarks of Any.do Inc., used with permission.

Moreover, below every email message in your Gmail account, there will be a **What's Next** tab that allows you to add tasks related to that email to your **Any.do** app right from your Gmail account. This is very useful, since once you are done reading an email, you can directly add tasks related to that email that you want to add to your list.

Any.do and the Any.do logo are registered trademarks of Any.do Inc., used with permission.

For example, maybe you need to follow up with the person who just emailed you and want to add a reminder to **Any.do**.

Using the **Any.do** app, you can keep all your tasks and to-do lists under control and send yourself reminders so that you can make sure you get them done.

13. HOW TO EASILY SPLIT THE BILL AT DINNER

< 120 Seconds

Billr and the Billr logo are the registered trademarks of Billr.Me: Bill Splitting at The Table., used with permission.

Have you ever witnessed chaos exploding at a restaurant table the moment the bill arrives and it needs to be split among a bunch of budget-conscious office colleagues or cash-crunched college buddies? Some people at the table ate only vegetarian food and don't want to pay for the non-vegetarian dishes. Some people at the table were teetotallers, while others guzzled down drinks like they were water. In the Indian context, it is not rare to have someone at the table keeping a special religious fast, who only ordered appropriately permitted food. The dilemma that engulfs everyone at the table is how to split the bill fairly so that no one at the table feels that they paid more than they should have.

There is a good iOS app called **Billr (http://billr.me)** that makes splitting the bill at a restaurant or bar among everyone at the table easy, fair and quick.

Start the **Billr** app on your iOS device and enter the number of people at the table among whom the bill needs to be split.

Billr and the Billr logo are the registered trademarks of Billr.Me: Bill Splitting at The Table., used with permission.

Next, you need to enter the prices of the items (drinks or food) that were ordered by specific people but not shared with anyone else at the table. You can either enter each item individually or enter a total amount that could be an approximation to save time.

Billr and the Billr logo are the registered trademarks of Billr.Me: Bill Splitting at The Table., used with permission.

In the next step, the **Billr** app will allow you to enter the prices for the items that were shared by more than one person at the table. Enter the prices of all the shared items that were ordered and also select all the people who shared each item.

Billr and the Billr logo are the registered trademarks of Billr.Me: Bill Splitting at The Table, used with permission.

Enter the tax and tip percentage that is applicable on the bill. **Billr** will proportionally split the tax and tip among everyone, based on the total value of items that each person individually ordered.

Billr will now calculate and display what each person at the table needs to pay. You can pass around your iOS device to everyone at the table so that they can see what they need to pay. **Billr** also allows you to share the calculation results with everyone at the table via text message or email.

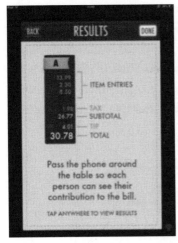
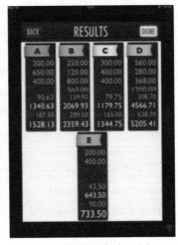

Billr and the Billr logo are the registered trademarks of Billr.Me: Bill Splitting at The Table, used with permission.

14. HOW TO CONVERT FILE FORMATS EASILY

 < 120 Seconds

In the war among various software and hardware companies, we are left with different file formats that open on certain devices and not on others. Unfortunately, it is the user who ultimately suffers. This makes it important to have your files in the right file formats; otherwise you may not be able to view or work with them. This is where file conversion can be so useful. Some common and popular file conversions are of your favourite songs, videos, documents and ebooks from one format to another.

All these file conversions and many more can be done in a matter of minutes on the free website **Zamzar (www.zamzar.com)**. No downloads or file installs are required.

Open your browser to **www.zamzar.com** and, in the **Step 1** box, select the file that you wish to convert. You can either upload a file from your computer or you can select a web URL where the file is located.

Zamzar and the Zamzar logo are registered trademarks of Zamzar Ltd, used with permission.

Now you need to select the format into which you want to convert the selected file. In this example, I am going to use **Zamzar** to convert a Word document into a PDF file.

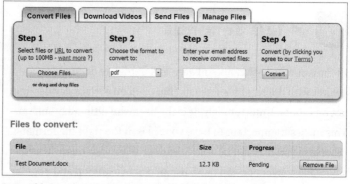

Zamzar and the Zamzar logo are registered trademarks of Zamzar Ltd, used with permission.

In the **Step 3** box, enter the email address where you wish to receive the converted file. Once you are ready to start the conversion process, click on the **Convert** button. The selected file will now be uploaded to the **Zamzar** server, and then converted to the desired format.

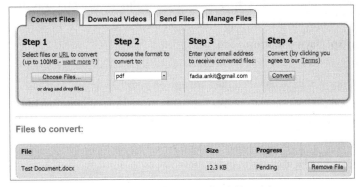

Zamzar and the Zamzar logo are registered trademarks of Zamzar Ltd, used with permission.

A few minutes later, when you check your email inbox, you would have received a link from **Zamzar** to the converted file.

15. HOW TO GET THE MOST OUT OF YOUR DAY

 < 120 Seconds

Do you often find yourself drowning in the deluge of information being thrown at you by your emails, calendars, social networks and online interactions? Wouldn't it be great if you had your very own online personal assistant who would go through all the information available at different places in your online world, organize everything in a useful format and present it to you so that you can make the most of your day?

Cue is a very useful app that connects to and indexes your online worlds (social networks, email accounts, calendars, online documents and others) and presents useful information in a nice format at the right time. Why spend time connecting to your different online accounts one by one, when the faster and more efficient thing to do is to simply use **Cue**? **Cue** is currently available as an app for the iOS platform and on the web from **http://www.cueup.com**.

Once you have installed the **Cue** app on your iOS device, you will need to link it to your online accounts. The more accounts you link to **Cue**, the more information it will be able to index and the more useful it will become. After linking your accounts, you will need to give it a few minutes to index them.

Once you have linked **Cue** to all your online accounts, it will show you the most relevant information from all your online worlds on a daily basis, so that you can make the most of your day. For example, you can see that below **Cue** has put together weather information, birthdays of Facebook friends and meetings scheduled for the day.

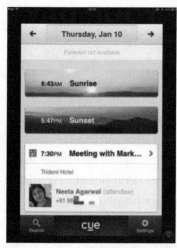 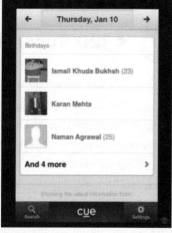

Cue and the Cue logo are registered trademarks of Greplin Inc., used with permission.

If you need directions to the meeting venue or if you are running late and want to drop a message to other attendees of the meeting, then simply select the meeting listed in the **Cue** app.

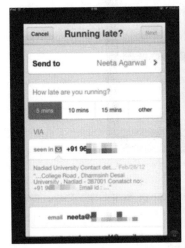

Cue and the Cue logo are registered trademarks of Greplin Inc., used with permission.

If you want a history of emails exchanged with any of the people attending the meeting, tap on their name on the screen and **Cue** will pull out the entire history of the interactions you have had with them in the past from all your different online worlds (email, social networks, calendars and others). This can be extremely useful in helping you prepare for your meeting. Moreover, **Cue** will pull up the selected person's professional work history from LinkedIn if you are connected there.

Cue will also show you any travel plan that you may have coming up, so that you can access all your travel details (flight information, hotel confirmations, car rentals etc.) right from your mobile phone or tablet device. With a single tap, you can even get directions from your current location to the airport.

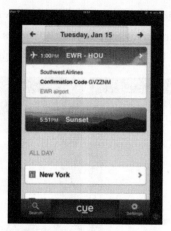

*Cue and the Cue logo are registered trademarks of
Greplin Inc., used with permission.*

Cue and the Cue logo are registered trademarks of Greplin Inc., used with permission.

Cue also has a powerful search function, which allows you to
quickly view a snapshot of all your interactions with particular
people across all your various online accounts.

Cue and the Cue logo are registered trademarks of Greplin Inc., used with permission.

16. HOW TO MANAGE, SEARCH AND SHARE YOUR FILE ATTACHMENTS

 < 360 Seconds

Managing the file attachments in your inbox can be quite a nightmare. While searching for a specific file, you need to remember who sent it to you, when it was sent and the subject of the email that contained it.

Attachments.me (https://attachments.me/) is a browser extension that plays the role of a file-attachment organizer and manager. **Attachments.me** will integrate with your Gmail account, making all file attachments in your email messages easily searchable. It will also allow you to create rules based on specific file attachment types and will automatically save them in your Google Drive. Moreover, **Attachments.me** also makes sharing your file attachments with others quite easy.

Attachments.me currently only works with Google Chrome and Mozilla Firefox, and only supports integration with a Gmail account. To install it, simply go to its website and click on the **Add** button.

Before the **Attachments.me** extension gets integrated with your Gmail account, it will ask for your permission. You don't need to worry about compromising the security and privacy of their Gmail account by installing **Attachments.me**.

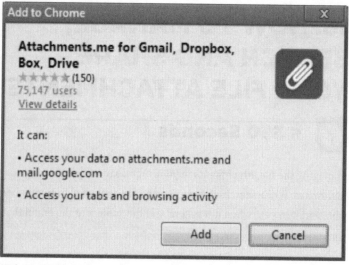

Attachments.me and the Attachments.me logo are registered trademarks of Attachments.me, used with permission.

The next time you open your Gmail account, **Attachments.me** will automatically start, and will allow you to set up the settings of how you want it to manage your email file attachments. Click on the

Click to get started button to start the configuration process, which takes only a few minutes.

Attachments.me and the Attachments.me logo are registered trademarks of Attachments.me, used with permission.

Attachments.me will ask for your permission to get access to your Gmail account to get the integration set-up. Click on the **Allow** button.

Attachments.me and the Attachments.me logo are registered trademarks of Attachments.me, used with permission.

Next, **Attachments.me** will ask you which online cloud account you want to use to save and manage your Gmail file attachments. I recommend integrating with Google Drive; however, you have a choice among Dropbox, Box, Google Drive and Sky Drive. Select the online cloud service of your choice and click on the **Link your account** button.

You will now be asked to give permission to **Attachments.me** to access your Google Drive. This is the last permission you need to give to **Attachments.me**, I promise!

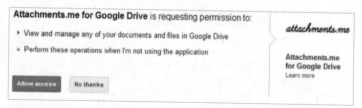

Attachments.me and the Attachments.me logo are registered trademarks of Attachments.me, used with permission.

When you see the message below on your screen, it means that **Attachments.me** has now been successfully integrated with your Google Drive.

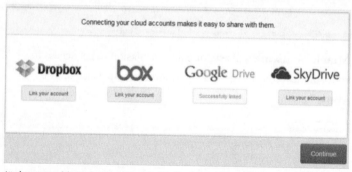

Attachments.me and the Attachments.me logo are registered trademarks of Attachments.me, used with permission.

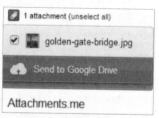

Attachments.me and the Attachments.me logo are registered trademarks of Attachments.me, used with permission.

Now that you have set up **Attachments.me** in your Gmail account and linked it to your Google Drive, whenever you receive an email with a file attachment, it will give you the option to save the attachment in any folder of your choice in your Google Drive.

You can save the file attachments to your Google Drive by creating automatic filing rules, or you can save them manually. When you log in to your Gmail account, you will notice a new **Attachments.me** icon in the top right corner, which allows you to manage all the settings related to it.

Automatic Filing Rules allow you to automatically save file attachments from your emails to a specific folder in your Google Drive account based on certain criteria (type of attachment, sender email address, subject of email and others). To create a new **Automatic Filing Rule**, all you need to do is click on the **Attachments.me** icon in your Gmail account > Click on **Automatic Filing Rules > Add New Rule**.

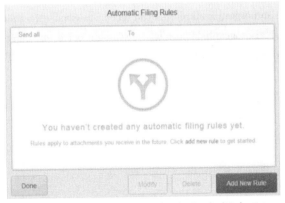

Attachments.me and the Attachments.me logo are registered trademarks of Attachments.me, used with permission.

You can also create a rule based on the sender's email address, the subject of the email, the name of the file attachment or even a keyword contained in the body of the email. You can create rules in such a manner that specific types of file attachments will be saved in specific folders on your Google Drive.

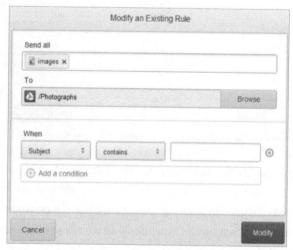

Attachments.me and the Attachments.me logo are registered trademarks of Attachments.me, used with permission.

To save and organize all photos you receive as email attachments in a special 'Photographs' folder in your Google Drive, you can create the following **Automatic Filing Rule**:

Attachments.me and the Attachments.me logo are registered trademarks of Attachments.me, used with permission.

Once you have created the **Automatic Filing Rule** of your choice
and started saving your file attachments in your Google Drive, it is also
very easy for you to quickly search through all your file attachments.
Simply connect your browser to **www.attachments.me**, or click on
the **Attachments.me** icon in your Gmail account and select the
Search Attachments option.

Attachments.me and the Attachments.me logo are registered trademarks of Attachments.me, used with permission.

The most useful feature of **Attachments.me** is that, while you are
composing a new email message, it allows you to upload a file
attachment directly from the online cloud (Google Drive or others). You
can also upload a file attachment from your computer, save it on your
Google Drive and send it as an email attachment—all in one step.

Overall, **Attachments.me** is a great app that gives you a lot of
power to efficiently organize, manage, search and share your file
attachments.

17. HOW TO MANAGE, SEARCH AND SHARE YOUR FILE ATTACHMENTS FROM A MOBILE PHONE

 < 360 Seconds

You are on the move and suddenly receive a call from your boss or client, asking you to email an important file. You don't have access to a computer and most smartphones have limited capabilities in terms of viewing, downloading and sending out attachments. In such situations, you either need to change your plans and rush to a computer or you are forced to delay the work until you do have access to a computer.

This is where the **Attachments.me** mobile app can be such a lifesaver. Before you proceed with this, I recommend that you make sure that you have read through and followed all the instructions provided in the previous tip.

The **Attachments.me** mobile app is currently available for the Android and iOS platforms and can be downloaded absolutely free of cost. It promises to make working with file attachments in your mailbox from your mobile phone a very easy and pain-free process.

Once you download, install and start the **Attachments.me** mobile app, you will need to log in to your Gmail account.

Attachments.me and the Attachments.me logo are registered trademarks of Attachments.me, used with permission.

We have already seen how to link **Attachments.me** with your Gmail and your Google Drive. Once you are logged in, you can use the **Attachments.me** app to have access to all the file attachments in all your Gmail messages and also in your Google Drive. There is a very convenient **Search** option that is available right at the top of the **Attachments.me** app and allows you to quickly search through all your file attachments. If you wish to email an attachment to someone, you can click on the **Compose** button on the top right corner of the app.

Attachments.me and the Attachments.me logo are registered trademarks of Attachments.me, used with permission.

You will now see the **Compose Mail** screen. You can type the **To:** email address, the subject and the body of the email. Finally, to attach a file to the email, simply click on the + sign.

Attachments.me will now give you the option to select a file to attach from your Google Drive or any other attachment from your inbox.

Attachments.me and the Attachments.me logo are registered trademarks of Attachments.me, used with permission.

I am selecting the option of choosing a file attachment from my Google Drive.

Attachments.me will now allow me to browse through all the files in my Google Drive, so that I can choose any file that I wish to attach to the email.

In case you chose the **Attach from Inbox** option, **Attachments.me** will show you all the file attachments from your inbox, so that you can choose any file that you wish to attach to the email.

Once you have selected the file that you wish to attach (from either your Gmail inbox or your Google Drive), all you need to do is to click on the **Send** button.

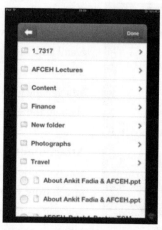

Attachments.me and the Attachments.me logo are registered trademarks of Attachments.me, used with permission.

18. HOW TO TAKE NOTES USING GMAIL

 < 300 Seconds

Spontaneous note-taking helps you remember something cool that you thought, heard or saw. It enables you to organize the chores you need to do at home. At the workplace, notes in the form of a to-do list can help you stay focused. Notes can be reminders of personal goals that you have set for yourself. You could also create a wish list of great restaurants or exotic holiday locations.

There are numerous note-taking apps that have been released in the last few years. However, one of the most effective in terms of user-friendliness is a free app called **Sticky (www.sticky.io)**.

Sticky completely integrates with Gmail and allows you to enter notes from within Gmail Chat or any other Google Talk messenger client installed on your computer, mobile or tablet.

> ## Welcome to Sticky!
> Sticky hooks right into your G-chat, please return to G-mail and accept the friend request. For example:

Sticky and the Sticky logo are registered trademarks of Sticky.io, used with permission.

Once you install Sticky, you will receive a friend request from **notes@sticky.io**. When you accept the friend request, you will be able to enter notes into **Sticky** from within any Google or Gmail Chat client just like you would send a chat message to a friend. No need to open any new app or window in your browser!

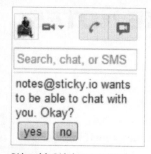

Sticky and the Sticky logo are registered trademarks of Sticky.io, used with permission.

Sticky is incredibly convenient because it allows you to use the at-sign (@) to enter notes into different notebooks and the hashtag (#) to classify the notes. For examples, you may want to enter your work notes in the @work notebook and home notes in the @home notebook. The use of the hashtag and the at-sign makes the process of entering notes very intuitive. At the same time, because of the pre-sorting that happens as you classify notes, it makes it very easy to search through your notes.

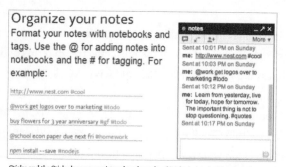

Sticky and the Sticky logo are registered trademarks of Sticky.io, used with permission.

Here are some examples of how you can enter different types of notes in **Sticky** using the Google Talk client or Gmail Chat:

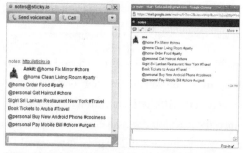

Sticky and the Sticky logo are registered trademarks of Sticky.io, used with permission.

Whenever you wish to view any of your saved notes, simply start a browser on your computer, phone or tablet and log in to **www.sticky.io** with your Gmail ID.

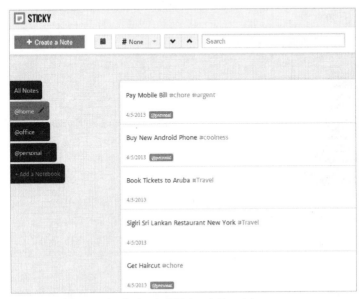

Sticky and the Sticky logo are registered trademarks of Sticky.io, used with permission.

Sticky and the Sticky logo are registered trademarks of Sticky.io, used with permission.

It is very easy to search for notes based on the hashtags, notebook names, the actual text inside notes or even the date on which the note was taken. For example, if you wish to view all notes that were hashtagged as #coolness, simply select the relevant hashtag from the drop-down list or search for #coolness in the discovery input search box.

Similarly, if you wish to view all notes from your home notebook, click on the relevant notebook in the left column or search for @ home in the discovery input search box.

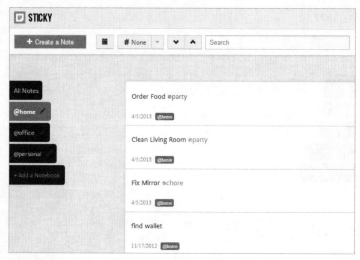

Sticky and the Sticky logo are registered trademarks of Sticky.io, used with permission.

It is possible to search for notes based on multiple rules as well. For example, you can search for all notes in the @home notebook with the hashtag #chore.

19. HOW TO PERMANENTLY DELETE FILES FROM YOUR COMPUTER, TABLET OR PHONE

 < 120 Seconds

Have there been occasions when you have sold, donated or discarded an old mobile phone, laptop or pen drive and simply deleted all the data on it—under the misconception that all of it has been permanently erased? Do you want to give away a used pen drive to a friend or relative, but would like to be sure that it does not have any of your old data on it? In this section we are going to learn how to completely, permanently delete data from all your various devices, so that no one can ever recover it.

Typically, whenever you delete any file or folder from your computer, pen drive or any other device, it is first sent to the recycle bin. This is easily recoverable. Unfortunately, even if you completely empty your recycle bin, it does not mean that the files have been permanently deleted. The deleted data remains on your hard drive in the form of dead files. There are sophisticated techniques available to recover these dead files from your computer.

This is why it is very important to permanently erase sensitive data from your hard drives. There is a free app called **Eraser (http://sourceforge.net/projects/eraser/)** that allows you to do just that. Once you have downloaded this app, all you need to do

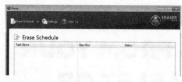

is to select the files or folders that you wish to permanently delete, and then let **Eraser** do the rest.

Eraser and the Eraser logo are registered trademarks of Eraser, used with permission.

To select the data you wish to permanently delete, click on the down arrow button next to **Erase Schedule** and then click on the **Add Data** button.

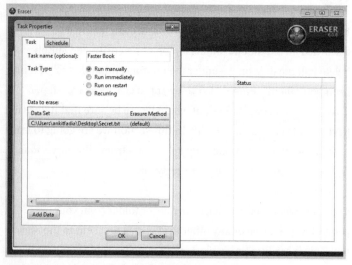

Eraser and the Eraser logo are registered trademarks of Eraser, used with permission.

Finally, once you have finished selecting the data that you wish to erase permanently, click on the **OK** button. Within a few seconds, **Eraser** will work its magic and permanently erase all the selected data. The way this works is that it shreds the last remains of deleted files by overwriting them with sophisticated patterns of useless data multiple times, hence making it impossible for anyone else to be able to recover it. Now that you know how to use **Eraser**, you can start deleting all the dirty secrets you have on your computer that you don't want anyone to ever find out.

20. HOW TO RECOVER DELETED FILES

 < 180 Seconds

Have you ever accidently deleted some memorable photos from your computer, camera or pen drive? Have you ever lost important files because of a system or software crash? Let us assume the worst case scenario—that you accidently deleted a file and then emptied your recycle bin as well. How do you recover the file now? In such situations, the ability to be able to recover deleted files could be a lifesaver.

Usually, once a file has also been deleted from the recycle bin, it can no longer be accessed by Windows, but still remains somewhere on your hard drive in the form of 'dead files'. Typically, such dead files remain on your drive for several days (sometimes even for weeks or months) until they are overwritten by new files or data that you create on your system. Luckily, such dead files, although considered inaccessible to the average user, can actually be recovered using data-recovery tools like **Recuva**, available as a free download from **http://www.piriform.com/recuva**. Once you realize that you have accidentally deleted or lost important data, it advisable that you start the recovery process as soon as possible, to prevent the deleted files from being overwritten accidentally.

Once you have installed **Recuva** on your system, the **Recuva Wizard** will automatically start. The interface of the **Recuva Wizard** makes it very simple and straightforward for you to recover your deleted files. Just follow the instructions on the screen and click on the **Next** button to continue.

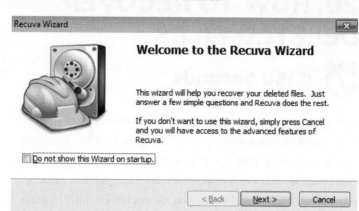

Recuva Wizard and the Recuva Wizard logo are registered trademarks of Piriform Ltd, used with permission.

At the next screen, you need to select the type of file you have accidentally deleted that you wish to recover and click on the **Next** button. The more specific you are in terms of the file information you provide to **Recuva**, the greater are your chances of being able to recover the files.

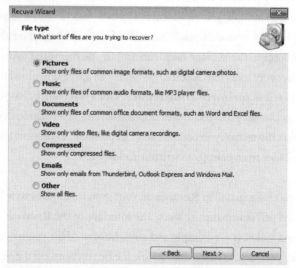

Recuva Wizard and the Recuva Wizard logo are registered trademarks of Piriform Ltd, used with permission.

Now you need to select the location where the files existed before they were deleted. You can choose a specific folder on your computer or external drive (hard drive, pen drive, camera or iPod), or even the entire system in case you have forgotten the exact location. Click on the **Next** button to continue.

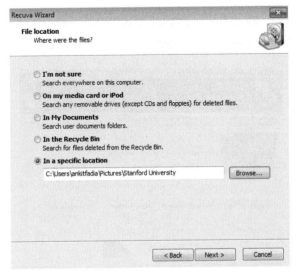

Recuva Wizard and the Recuva Wizard logo are registered trademarks of Piriform Ltd, used with permission.

Recuva will now search for all available dead files in the folder that you selected. Typically the scan does not take more than a few seconds.

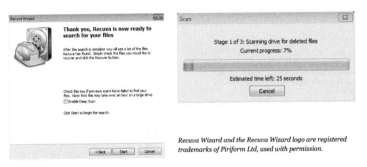

Recuva Wizard and the Recuva Wizard logo are registered trademarks of Piriform Ltd, used with permission.

Once **Recuva** has found the dead files, it will analyse them to figure out how damaged they are. If the dead files have already been overwritten by new files, it may not be possible to recover them. Otherwise, most of the dead files that are found will be easily recovered.

You need to now select the files you wish to recover from the list of dead files that **Recuva** finds, and then click on the **Recover** button.

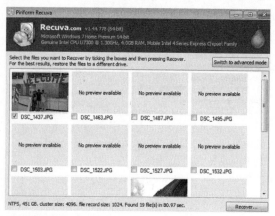

Recuva Wizard and the Recuva Wizard logo are registered trademarks of Piriform Ltd, used with permission.

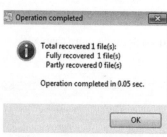

Recuva Wizard and the Recuva Wizard logo are registered trademarks of Piriform Ltd, used with permission.

Within a few seconds, **Recuva** will recover the selected dead files, and will allow you to save them anywhere on your computer. It is recommended that after recovering the files, you should save them in a drive other than the place where the original files were located. Once you install **Recuva** on your computer, you can delete your files fearlessly because you know you can get them back.

21. HOW TO MAKE LIFE SIMPLER BY AUTOMATING TASKS ON YOUR MOBILE PHONE

 < 360 Seconds

Usually, you need to manually give your mobile phone instructions by pressing keys or selecting options on it. Wouldn't it be great, instead, if you could teach your phone to automatically do things for you whenever certain predefined conditions were fulfilled?

Tasker is a task-automation app that allows you to teach or programme your phone to automatically perform tasks for you when certain conditions are fulfilled. For example, **Tasker** can be a lifesaver if you want to go to bed early, but want your phone to automatically send a text message birthday greeting to your friend at midnight. It is currently available only for Android phones and can be downloaded for approximately $7 from the Google Play App Store.

Before you start using the **Tasker** app to transform your Android phone, it is important for you to understand the following terms:

Term	Definition
Action	A function that the **Tasker** app can perform on your phone. For example, sending an SMS message, switching off Wi-Fi and so on
Task	A collection of actions that can be performed on your phone
Context / Event	The trigger point when reached that leads to the execution of a task
Profile	A collection of tasks that will be executed when it is enabled
Exit Task	A task that is executed when the profile has finished performing its task and the context is no longer valid

The first time you run **Tasker**, you need to press the + button to create a new profile for the group of automatic tasks you want to activate on your phone. In this example, I am going to automate a task containing the action of sending a birthday wish via SMS to a friend at the predefined time (context) of 00.00 hrs.

Tasker and the Tasker logo are registered trademarks of Tasker, used with permission.

Enter a name for the new profile and press the **Tick** button. In this case, I am going to name the profile 'My First Profile'.

Tasker will now ask you to choose a **Context** or **Trigger** event, which, when fulfilled, will tell your phone to perform the automated task. There are a number of contexts or triggers that can be used in **Tasker**, and it is highly recommended that you invest some time to get familiar with

Tasker and the Tasker logo are registered trademarks of Tasker, used with permission.

them. For example, the context can be a particular date or time, the start or exit of a particular app, your GPS location, some hardware or software state of your phone (when you plug in your headphones or dock your phone), or even some event that takes place on your phone (when you receive a phone call or a text message).

Tasker and the Tasker logo are registered trademarks of Tasker, used with permission.

Tasker and the Tasker logo are registered trademarks
of Tasker, used with permission.

I want to wish my friend at midnight, so I am going to set the **Context/Trigger** to the condition that the action is performed at midnight.

Tasker will now ask you to create a **New Task** that you want to perform. This task will be automatically executed whenever the trigger condition or context is fulfilled. Press the **New Task** option and enter a name for the new task and tap the tick button. In this example, I am going to name the task 'Birthday Message'.

Tasker and the Tasker logo are registered trademarks of Tasker, used with permission.

Now you need to tap the + button to add a new action to the task 'Birthday Message'. Tasker supports a vast variety of actions that can be performed on your phone. Once again, it is highly recommended that you explore all these possible actions.

Tasker and the Tasker logo are registered trademarks of Tasker, used with permission.

In this example, the action that I want to perform is to send a birthday greeting message to my friend via SMS text message. To select this particular action, I am going to press **Phone** > **Send SMS**.

Tasker will now ask you to enter the message body and destination number for the SMS text message you want to send. Press the **Tick** button to continue.

Tasker and the Tasker logo are registered trademarks of Tasker, used with permission.

At this stage, in case they are required, you can choose to add more actions to your task by pressing the + button. If you do not want to add any other action to this task, simply press the **Tick** button.

The automated task of sending the birthday message via SMS at the specified time (midnight) has now been set up on your Android phone. You can go to sleep and rest assured your phone will do the rest.

Tasker and the Tasker logo are registered trademarks of Tasker, used with permission.

This was just a simple example of what you can do with the **Tasker** app. There are many useful automated tasks that you can perform on your Android phone. For example, you can:

1. Start your music player automatically whenever your headphones are connected

Using **Tasker**, it is possible to automate your Android phone in such a manner that, whenever you plug in your headphones, your phone will automatically launch the music player of your choice.

Context: State > Hardware > Headset Plugged
Action: App > Load App > Choose App of your Choice

Tasker and the Tasker logo are registered trademarks of Tasker, used with permission.

Tasker and the Tasker logo are registered trademarks of Tasker, used with permission.

2. Switch on the GPS feature whenever navigation apps are started and switch it off on exit

If you keep the GPS feature of your phone switched on all the time, it will end up eating up valuable battery life. If you wish to conserve your battery life, it is a good idea to use **Tasker** to automatically switch on GPS only when you launch an app that requires GPS to function.

Context: Application > Choose all the Navigation Apps you want
Action: Misc > GPS > On
Exit Task: Misc > GPS > Off

3. Conserve your battery when it becomes low

Whenever your battery is low, it is possible to use Tasker to automatically make certain changes on your phone so that your battery life is conserved.

Context: State > Power > Battery > Choose a battery level of your choice using the slide bars.
In this example, I am choosing the range 0–20.

Action: Net > Wi-Fi > Off
Action: Display > Display Brightness > Reduce the level of your choice.
Action: Misc > GPS > Off

Action: Net > Auto-Sync > Off
Action: Net > Mobile Data > Off
Action: Net > Airplane mode > On

4. Automatically send an SMS to callers whose calls you miss
If you are busy and cannot answer a call, you use **Tasker** to
automatically send an SMS to any caller whose calls you may have
missed, with a predefined message of your choice.

Context: State > Phone > Missed Call
Action: Phone > Send SMS > Press the Variable button > Select
the variable 'Caller Number (In)', which will be %CNUM in this
case > Type the body of the SMS you want to send to the caller.

Tasker and the Tasker logo are registered trademarks of Tasker, used with permission.

Instead of sending an SMS text message to all callers whose calls
you have missed, you can configure **Tasker** to only send the SMS in
case of a missed call from a certain number.

Context: State > Phone > Missed Call > Enter the number of caller. Action: Phone > Send SMS > Enter the number of the caller > Type the body of the SMS you want to send to the caller.

5. Turn your phone to silent when it is placed face down

If you are in a meeting, it is possible for you to configure **Tasker** in such a manner that your mobile phone will automatically turn to silent mode whenever it is placed with its face down. Whenever your phone is kept in the face-up mode, the ringer volume and notification volume will go back to their normal levels.

Context: State > Sensor > Orientation > Face Down
Action: Audio Settings > Ringer Volume > Set it to 0.
Action: Audio Settings > Notification Volume > Set it to 0.
Exit Action: Audio Settings > Ringer Volume > Set it to 5.
Exit Action: Audio Settings > Notification Volume > Set it to 5.

Tasker and the Tasker logo are registered trademarks of Tasker, used with permission.

6. Enable Wi-Fi whenever you are at home

Whenever you reach home, you can configure **Tasker** to automatically enable Wi-Fi on your phone, so that you can save some money on your data plan.

Context: State > Phone > Cell Near > Click on Scan. Your phone will now scan for mobile towers nearby. Make sure you are at home when you perform the scan. Walk around your house so that all the mobile towers that are nearby get recorded by your mobile phone.
Action: Net > WiFi > On

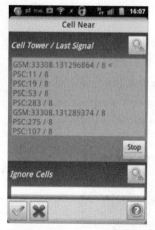 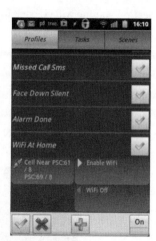

Tasker and the Tasker logo are registered trademarks of Tasker, used with permission.

7. Execute tasks on your phone by shaking it

It is possible to perform predefined tasks on your phone by simply shaking it. For example, you can configure **Tasker** to call a predefined number whenever you shake it in a particular manner.

Context: Event > Sensor > Shake > Choose the type of shake.
Action: Phone > Call > Enter the number you want to call.

Tasker and the Tasker logo are registered trademarks of Tasker, used with permission.

8. Control your phone remotely via SMS

It is possible for you to remotely control your mobile phone by sending an SMS text message to it. For example, you can send a text message to your phone to take a photograph using the camera on your phone.

Context: Event > Phone > Received Text > Select SMS in the Type Field, type the mobile phone number from where you want to send the SMS command in the Sender field and finally in the Content field type any command of your choice. For example, in this case I am going to type 'photo' in the **Content** field. **Action: Media > Take Photo > Enable Discreet if you want to secretly take the photo.** Select whatever other options (like file name, flash setting, type of photograph and others) you want related to the photo.

With the **Tasker** app on your Android phone, you can automate a lot of tasks and let your mobile phone do them for you.

Tasker and the Tasker logo are registered trademarks of Tasker, used with permission.

22. HOW TO CREATE EXPENSE REPORTS EASILY

 < 120 Seconds

Have you ever lost money because you lost expense receipts and could not claim the reimbursement from your office? Does your company have strict expense reimbursement policies that you find cumbersome? With the **Expensify** app on your mobile phone, filing expense reports at work and claiming reimbursement for them become a breeze. No need to scan your receipts to your computer and no need to buy expensive accounting software!

The **Expensify** app can be accessed via the web at **www.expensify.com** and downloaded to your smartphone (Android, iOS, BlackBerry, Windows etc.). The interface of **Expensify** is very clean, uncluttered and intuitive, which makes filing expense reports hassle-free. It allows you to create expense reports directly from your mobile phone while you are on the move.

Expensify and the Expensify logo are registered trademarks of Expensify Inc., used with permission.

Once you launch **Expensify** on your mobile phone, the first step is to create a new expense report. On the bottom of the home screen of the **Expensify** app, press **Reports** > **New** > Enter a report name of your choice. Once you have created a report, you can add as many expense receipts to it as you want. In this example, I am going to create a new expense report called 'Delhi client meeting'.

The best thing about **Expensify** is that it allows you to take a photo of your receipts while you are on the move, so that you never lose them. You can then manually enter the important fields like merchant name, price, date, type of expense and other details. To add an expense to a particular expense report, simply tap the (unreported) field and choose the relevant expense from the list.

Expensify and the Expensify logo are registered trademarks of Expensify Inc., used with permission.

Expensify and the Expensify logo are registered trademarks of Expensify Inc., used with permission.

In this example, I have taken a photo of my bill at Burger Place and added it to the 'Delhi client meeting' expense report. Using the **SmartScan** feature, you can automatically scan a receipt by taking a photo of it using the camera on your phone. This feature is really useful since it saves you the time and hassle of having to manually type the various values from receipts. Instead, let **Expensify's SmartScan** feature do it for you. You get ten free scans

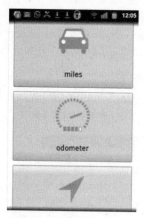

Expensify and the Expensify logo are registered trademarks of Expensify, Inc., used with permission.

Expensify and the Expensify logo are registered trademarks of Expensify Inc., used with permission.

every month, after which you need to pay 20 cents per scan.

If you are using your personal car for work purposes and your company is supposed to reimburse your fuel expenses, the **Mileage** feature in **Expensify** makes it very easy for you to file your claims. Depending upon what your company requires, you can either create a fuel expense report based on the number of miles (or kilometres) you have travelled, or based on your odometer readings, or even by switching on the GPS feature of your phone and letting it record the distance you have travelled.

If you are a consultant and are paid by the hour, the **Time** feature in the **Expensify** app makes it very easy for you to clock your hours and claim reimbursement for them.

Once you have added all the expenses to your expense report, you can submit it to relevant people in your office for processing. Go to the home screen of the **Expensify** app > Tap on **Reports** > Tap on the report you wish to submit > Tap on **Submit**. You will be asked to enter the email addresses to which you want to submit the expense report. Press the **Submit** button and **Expensify** will email the expense report for you!

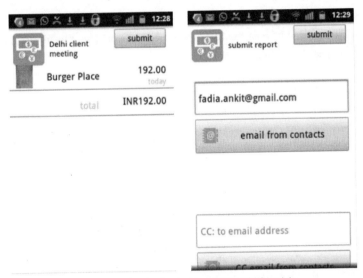

Expensify and the Expensify logo are registered trademarks of Expensify Inc., used with permission.

Typically, the expense report that is sent will contain a list of your expenses in tabular format and also the photos of the original receipts as supporting evidence.

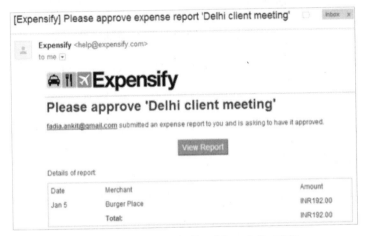

Expensify and the Expensify logo are registered trademarks of Expensify Inc., used with permission.

For example, below is an email from **Expensify** containing the expense report I was creating. The expense report contains my expenses in a tabular format.

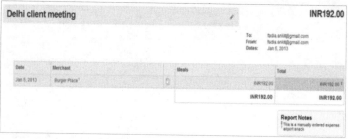

Expensify and the Expensify logo are registered trademarks of Expensify Inc., used with permission.

It also contains the photos of my receipts.

Expensify and the Expensify logo are registered trademarks of Expensify Inc., used with permission.

The concerned person at your office has the option to approve or reject your expense report with a single mouse click. Once approved, **Expensify** also allows the reimbursement to be made via a direct bank deposit or PayPal.

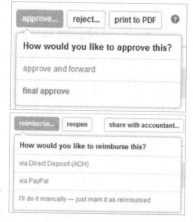

Expensify and the Expensify logo are registered trademarks of Expensify Inc., used with permission.

23. HOW TO DRIVE SAFELY WITH THE HELP OF YOUR PHONE

 < 120 Seconds

When we are constantly connected and always communicating with the rest of the world, some of us begin to feel a little uneasy when we can't do so, for example, while driving a car. Talking on the phone without using a Bluetooth hands-free device is not the safest thing to do, but, unfortunately, it has become a common sight on roads across the world. Reading and replying to text messages or emails while driving are even more dangerous. Not only does it distract you, it also takes one hand away from the steering wheel. Research has revealed that a large number of road accidents occur due to driving while messaging, emailing and chatting on smartphones.

There is a good tool that will make driving safer for you and your family members. **DriveSafe.ly** is a free mobile app that you can download from **http://www.drivesafe.ly**. It runs on most popular smartphone platforms like Android, iOS and BlackBerry.

Once installed, you can switch the app on and off as per your convenience. Now, if you receive any email or a text message while driving, **DriveSafe.ly** will read it out aloud to you in a voice of your choice!

DriveSafe.ly and the DriveSafe.ly logo are registered trademarks of iSpeech Inc., used with permission.

This ensures that your hands can be on the steering wheel instead of on your phone and, at the same time, you don't end up missing any important text messages or emails. You can hear all the incoming messages, either directly from the speaker of the mobile phone or through the Bluetooth earpiece. The application also allows you to configure an auto response that will automatically be sent out whenever you receive a message, alerting people that you are driving and will get back to them as soon as possible.

There is a premium version of this app available, known as **DriveSafe.ly Pro**, which even allows you to reply to any received email or text message by simply speaking into your mobile phone. There are numerous subscription packages that you can choose from, based on your requirements.

DriveSafe.ly and the DriveSafe.ly logo are registered trademarks of iSpeech Inc., used with permission.

24. HOW TO SEND STUFF FROM YOUR BROWSER TO YOUR MOBILE DEVICE

 < 60 Seconds

Have you ever been reading an interesting article online in the browser on your office computer, and wished that there was a way to continue reading it on your mobile or tablet when you left the office? Have you ever looked up directions to some place on Google Maps on your computer and wanted to send them to your mobile or tablet so that you could access them while you are in the car? In such situations, the obvious thing to do is to email the URL web address of the web page to your own account. There is an easier method.

Google Chrome and the Google Chrome logo are registered trademarks of Google Inc., used with permission.

Using the **Google Chrome** browser, it is possible for you to sign in to your Google account, so that any open tabs, bookmarks, apps and browser preferences that you have get automatically synced across all your devices (computers, mobile phones and tablets). This will eliminate the need to email links to yourself. Please note that most modern-day browsers like Mozilla Firefox also support this functionality.

To do this, start **Google Chrome** on your computer, click on the **Settings** button and then select the **Sign in to Chrome** option.

You will be asked to log in to your Google account so that all the open tabs, apps, bookmarks and browser preferences in your **Google Chrome** can be automatically saved to your Google account and synced across all your devices.

Once you have signed in to **Google Chrome** on your computer, you can click on the **Advanced** link > **Advanced sync settings** button to manage the various settings related to the browser auto-sync feature.

Google Chrome and the Google Chrome logo are registered trademarks of Google Inc., used with permission.

To get maximum benefit out of the auto-sync feature, make sure you install the **Google Chrome** browser on all your mobile phones and tablet devices and enable the **Sync** option on all them by signing in to your Google account.

Once the syncing feature has been enabled across all your devices, you can make full use of the auto-sync functionality. With it enabled, you will be able to automatically see the same page on your mobile phone, tablet and home computer. Simply start the **Google Chrome** browser in any of your devices and select the **Other devices** tab in the bottom bar of the browser.

This will display all the tabs that are currently open—or were open when the last sync happened—in **Google Chrome** on all your other devices, hence allowing you to access them easily and quickly. Not only can you use this option to access open tabs from one remote computer, you can also use it to access open tabs from all the multiple computers, devices and tablets that you are own. Just remember to sign in to your Google account and enable the auto-sync feature on all of them.

The reverse is also possible. If you open some tabs in **Google Chrome** on your tablet or mobile device, you will be able to access it from your office computer! For example, if you open a newspaper article in the **Google Chrome** browser on your tablet or mobile device, from your computer you can automatically access the same page.

By auto-syncing your tabs, bookmarks, apps and browser preferences across all your devices, you can share content between them easily and quickly.

25. HOW TO MAKE WEB PAGES PRINT-FRIENDLY

 < 60 Seconds

Whenever you print an article from a website, a lot of junk in the form of images, advertisements, and navigation links also gets printed. This not only makes the printed pages appear very cluttered and unprofessional, but also ends up wasting a lot of paper and ink. This is why a very useful app called **PrintFriendly (http://www.printfriendly.com)** exists. This app cleans all the junk from web pages and gives you a clean printed page.

To use **PrintFriendly**, simply start your browser and connect to its website **http://www.printfriendly.com** and, in the space provided, enter the web address or URL of the web page you wish to print cleanly.

PrintFriendly and the PrintFriendly logo are registered trademarks of PrintFriendly, used with permission.

Click on the **Print Preview** button to display a clean version of the web page that you want to print. When you do this, **PrintFriendly** will remove all ads, images and navigation bars which are normally present on the page. You can either print the page directly at this stage, or choose to save it as a PDF file so that you can view and print it later on. You can also choose to change the font size of the text on this page to suit your preferences.

PrintFriendly and the PrintFriendly logo are registered trademarks of PrintFriendly, used with permission.

It is also possible to integrate **PrintFriendly** into most popular browsers like Google Chrome, Firefox, Internet Explorer and others. This will ensure that you can make use of the benefits of **PrintFriendly** with a single click of the mouse and do not need to keep visiting the **PrintFriendly** website each time you want to print something.

26. HOW TO TYPE FASTER ON A TOUCHSCREEN ANDROID DEVICE

 **< 120 seconds**

A common complaint about using touchscreen devices is that it slows down your typing speed as compared to a phone with a traditional keyboard. Have you ever wanted to unleash your typing skills so that you can type faster and better on your touchscreen Android phone than ever before?

SwiftKey is a very useful Android app that learns your writing style, adapts to it and allows you to type faster and more accurately on your touchscreen Android device by predicting and auto-correcting what you are typing. Usually, while you are typing on your mobile device, you can either input text normally or using the T9 predictive text functionality. Think of **SwiftKey** as a much more evolved, improved and smarter version of T9 predictive text.

SwiftKey can be downloaded from **http://www.swiftkey. net** for approximately $1, and is arguably one of the best apps you will ever buy for your Android device. **SwiftKey** makes use of the openness of Android to take control of the keyboard function of your device and make it work much better than before. It is currently available only for Android users.

Once you download **SwiftKey** on your Android device, during the installation process, it will replace the default keyboard style being used by your device with the **SwiftKey** keyboard. It may seem a little complicated at first, but just follow the instructions on the screen and everything will fall into place.

SwiftKey and the SwiftKey logo are registered trademarks of TouchType Ltd, used with permission.

Some of the wonderful features available in the **SwiftKey** app are the following:

1. Word prediction technology
SwiftKey makes use of a very powerful and accurate word prediction technology that analyses what you have typed so far, searches its own internal database to figure out how sentences like yours are framed by others and predicts what you are going to type next even before you actually start typing it. For example, I was typing the text 'Why are you' and it automatically predicted the next possible words as 'doing', 'going' or 'waiting'. It doesn't end there—out of the predicted words, it displayed the most likely (or most commonly used) word in the middle and highlighted it, making it very easy for me to pick it without actually having to type it out.

SwiftKey and the SwiftKey logo are registered trademarks of TouchType Ltd, used with permission.

2. Space prediction technology

If you forget to type a space between consecutive words, **SwiftKey** is still able to figure out what you are typing. For example, 'Whatsreyoudoubgtobught' automatically becomes 'What are you doing tonight'. In other words, **SwiftKey's** space prediction technology allows you to type without using spaces!

SwiftKey and the SwiftKey logo are registered trademarks of TouchType Ltd, used with permission.

SwiftKey and the SwiftKey logo are registered trademarks of TouchType Ltd, used with permission.

3. Spelling correction

It will automatically correct any mistyped or misspelled words for you on the fly as you type.

SwiftKey and the v logo are registered trademarks of TouchType Ltd, used with permission.

4. Personalization to your writing style

The best thing about **SwiftKey** is that it can adapt and learn your personalized writing style by going through your posts on Facebook, your Gmail account, your tweets and so on. For example, if you use some phrases or slang regularly in your email account, the next time you are typing it on your Android device, **SwiftKey** will be able to predict it as soon as you start typing.

5. Continuous learning

The more you type using **SwiftKey**, the better it will understand your writing style and adapt to it.

6. Long Press

When you long-press the period key, **SwiftKey** will automatically predict the most commonly used punctuation marks, making it easier for you to type punctuation marks.

7. Support for 54 languages

SwiftKey supports input in various languages.

8. SwiftKey Flow

The most exciting development from the **SwiftKey** team is the release of **SwiftKey Flow** beta version (available from **http://www.swiftkey.net/flow/**), which promises to transform the way we type on our touchscreen devices. It allows you to type an entire sentence without even once lifting your fingers off the screen. It is almost as if you are swiping instead of typing.

Apps that also allow you to type faster on your touchscreen mobile devices are:

▶ **Swype (http://www.swype.com)**

▶ **8Pen (http://www.8pen.com).**

27. HOW TO FIGHT SPAM IN YOUR GMAIL ACCOUNT

 < 120 Seconds

According to reports, more than 90 per cent of all email being sent over the Internet is spam. The good news for **Gmail** users is that **Gmail** does a much better job of fighting spam than most other email service providers out there. If you are using **Gmail**, chances are that most spam messages do not even make it to your inbox. However, in the odd case that spam emails do make it through **Gmail's** filters, there are a few simple things you can do to fight it.

Any email that you may have received in your inbox can be reported as spam to **Gmail** by simply clicking on the **Report Spam** button found above the opened email. It is a good practice to report the spam message to **Gmail**, rather than simply deleting it, since it helps **Gmail** grow its database of known types of spam messages.

Gmail and the Gmail logo are registered trademarks of Google Inc., used with permission.

If you notice that you are receiving the same spam message over and over again, it is also possible for you to take more serious steps to counter it. Maybe you are receiving the same marketing email from the same company every single day. Or maybe you are winning the same lottery in Nigeria every other day. In such cases, it is highly recommended that you create a filtering rule to automatically delete such messages even before they appear in your inbox.

To create a filtering rule, simply open the spam message you have received, click on the **More** button and then select the **Filter messages like these** option.

Gmail and the Gmail logo are registered trademarks of Google Inc., used with permission.

Gmail will automatically analyse the spam message and create a filter based on the email address at which the spam message had originated. You may modify the filter if you want and, once you are done, simply click on the **Create filter with this search** option at the bottom right corner.

Gmail and the Gmail logo are registered trademarks of Google Inc., used with permission.

Gmail will now ask you what action you would like to perform when email messages matching the filtering rule are received in your inbox. In this case, since we are trying to fight spam, I suggest selecting the **Delete it** option. This will ensure that any future email you get from the email address will automatically be deleted without even appearing in your inbox. You can use this technique to fight spam, block unsolicited marketing emails or even reject messages from an annoying ex!

Gmail and the Gmail logo are registered trademarks of Google Inc., used with permission

There is also another way of fighting spam—disposable email addresses. A number of websites ask you for your email address for registration, verification or other purposes. Unfortunately, there is no way to tell if they will end up spamming your email account or not. This is where disposable email addresses in **Gmail** come into the picture.

One of the lesser known facts about **Gmail** is that if your email address is user@gmail.com, any email sent to user+something@gmail.com will also automatically get delivered to your real email account user@gmail.com. You can create as many disposable email addresses you want with creative names of your choice without even officially registering them with **Gmail**. Try it out! The reason why these disposable email addresses work is that **Gmail** basically ignores everything after the + sign and before the @ sign in your email address.

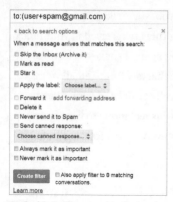

Gmail and the Gmail logo are registered trademarks of Google Inc., used with permission.

This means that if you are worried that a particular website may end up spamming you or misusing your email address, it makes sense to give them a disposable email address (like user+spam@gmail.com) instead of your real email address (user@gmail.com). Such a strategy will ensure that you can still receive legitimate emails from the website, since all emails sent to your disposable email address will come to you. In case the website ends up spamming you, you can just set up a filter in your Gmail account to automatically delete all emails sent to user+spam@gmail.com without them even showing up in your inbox.

28. HOW TO SHARE STUFF ONLINE EASILY AND QUICKLY

 < 60 seconds

If you wish to share an interesting web page with someone else, you have to copy the web address, open your email account or a social networking site (Facebook, Gmail, Yahoo or others), paste the web address and then hit the send or share button. There is an easier and faster way called **Shareaholic**.

Shareaholic is an extension that is supported by most popular browsers (Google Chrome, Mozilla Firefox, Internet Explorer, Opera and others) and can be downloaded for free from **https://www.shareaholic.com/**. The only thing you need to do is to create an account before you can start using this service.

Shareaholic allows you to quickly share links across popular platforms like email (Gmail, Yahoo, Hotmail, AOL and others), social networking (Twitter, Facebook, Google+, Orkut and others), bookmarking sites (Delicious, StumbleUpon and others), blogs etc.

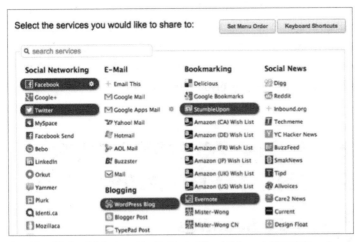

Shareaholic and the Shareaholic logo are registered trademarks of Shareaholic Inc., used with permission.

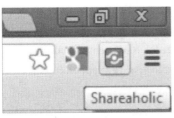

Shareaholic and the Shareaholic logo are registered trademarks of Shareaholic Inc., used with permission.

Once installed, **Shareaholic** will appear in the form of a new button next to the URL address bar in your browser. Whenever you are viewing a web page that you like a lot and want to share with the world, click on the **Shareaholic** button in your browser.

Shareaholic and the Shareaholic logo are registered trademarks of Shareaholic Inc., used with permission.

Shareaholic will display all the available platforms using which you can share the link or web page with your contacts. Select any platform you would like to use from the list displayed by **Shareaholic**.

For example, I wish to share a newspaper article with my friends using Facebook and Gmail. All I need to do is open that newspaper article in my browser, click on the **Shareaholic** button and then select Gmail and Facebook. Within a few seconds, **Shareaholic** will open new tabs in my browser which will allow me to instantly share the web page with anyone of my choice.

29. HOW TO USE YOUR PHONE TO BE PUNCTUAL

 < 60 Seconds

Do you have trouble making it to your meetings and appointments on time? With **Bounce** on your phone, you can make use of technology to tell you when it is time for you to leave from your current location, so that you make it to your next appointment location on time.

Bounce is an app that is currently available for both the Android and the iOS platforms. Once installed on your mobile phone, **Bounce** keeps track of your GPS location, the times and locations of the appointments listed in your calendar and live traffic data en route to your appointment locations, so that it can give you timely reminders to leave on time and not be late.

Bounce and the Bounce logo are registered trademarks of Bounce, used with permission.

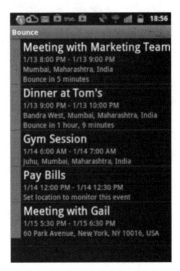

Bounce and the Bounce logo are registered trademarks of Bounce, used with permission.

You can go into **Settings** and configure how long before leaving you would like to be reminded. It is also possible for you to add buffer time for things like parking, walking to the car etc.

30. HOW TO EXTEND YOUR MOBILE PHONE'S BATTERY LIFE

 < 180 Seconds

Does your battery run out quickly and not even last you a full workday? Do you want to increase the battery life of your mobile phone, so that you can get more done each day? It is highly recommended that you implement these popular battery-saving strategies on your mobile device to increase its battery life:

1. Disable notifications that you don't need

2. Disable location services

3. Reduce the brightness of your screen

4. Reduce the auto-lock time to the minimum possible value

5. Turn off Wi-Fi

6. Turn off Bluetooth

7. Turn off push email/Internet access on your phone

8. Close applications that may be running in the background and eating up your battery charge.

On iOS devices, double-press the home screen button and hold your finger down on any icon on the screen until all of them start wriggling and then you can press the minimize button to close the apps running in the background. On Android devices, go to **Settings > Applications** > manually select and shut down all the apps that you are not using.

However, the problem with these battery-saving strategies is that most of them require you to manually change settings on your mobile phone and tend to interfere with your regular phone usage.

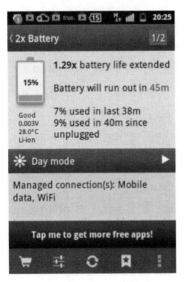

2x Battery Saver and the 2x Battery Saver logo are registered trademarks of Ao Soft Inc., used with permission.

Instead, there are numerous battery-management apps available that can help improve the battery life of your mobile phone by automatically implementing battery-saving strategies whenever you are not using your mobile phone.

If you want to increase the battery life of your Android phone, you can download the **2X Battery Saver** app to your phone for free from the Google Play App Store. First of all, **2X Battery Saver** always displays the battery level, usage and estimated battery life remaining in the status bar on your mobile screen, so that you can constantly keep track of it.

More importantly, **2X Battery Saver** helps increase the battery life of your phone by automatically switching off the Internet feature (3G, 4G and Wi-Fi) whenever your screen is locked. The constant use of Internet access by your phone—even when you are not using it—can drain your battery quite quickly. If you have your phone in your pocket and are not working on it, **2X Battery Saver** will kick in, switch off the Internet and conserve your battery charge.

The best part about this app is that it only shuts off the Internet
access on your phone and does not affect your phone calls and
text messages. To ensure that you do not lose out on any of your
important work (emails, news updates, instant messages etc.),
this app will keep enabling the Internet access on your phone
at predefined periodic intervals of your choice. Moreover, it is
designed in such a way that it will not switch off the Internet on
your phone if any active downloads are detected.

 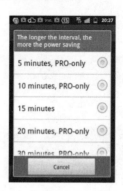

2x Battery Saver and the 2x Battery Saver logo are registered trademarks of Ao
Soft Inc., used with permission.

It is possible for you to configure **2X Battery Saver** to be
automatically enabled only when your battery charge becomes
lower than a particular level. Until that threshold is reached, your
phone will work normally. Why worry about saving your battery
when you don't need to? Moreover, the battery-saving feature is
automatically disabled whenever your phone is being charged at a
power source.

Another fantastic app that increases the battery life of your Android
phone by intelligently managing the features that eat your battery
charge is **JuiceDefender**. You can download it for free from the
Google Play App Store.

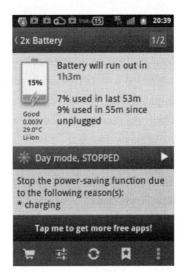

2x Battery Saver and the 2x Battery Saver logo are registered trademarks of Ao Soft Inc., used with permission.

For iOS users, one of the best battery-management apps is the **Battery Doctor Pro**, which is available for only 99 cents in the App Store. Once installed on your iOS device, **Battery Doctor** shows you the status of your battery charge and estimates how long your battery charge will last under different usage conditions like talk time, Internet access, YouTube playback, audio playback and others.

Battery Doctor and the Battery Doctor Logo are registered trademarks of Game Lingo LLC, used with permission.

When you press the **Inspection** button, **Battery Doctor** inspects your iOS device and figures out ways to increase your battery life by changing certain settings on your phone. It also displays the estimated battery charge increase if the recommended changes are implemented. The only limitation is that you will need to manually change the recommended settings, since iOS does not allow apps to make these changes.

The best feature of **Battery Doctor** is that it allows you to perform a full-cycle charge of your battery so that your iOS device can get a more accurate reading and your battery charge can be increased. It is recommended that you perform a full-cycle charge on your iOS device at least once a month.

31. HOW TO SCHEDULE STUFF WITH YOUR FRIENDS AND COLLEAGUES EASILY

 < 270 Seconds

Finding a mutually convenient date and time to schedule meetings with colleagues and clients can sometimes be more challenging than it needs to be. Even scheduling a fun night out with your friends can involve conference calls and many confusing emails, with everyone having different time commitments and preferences. Start using **Doodle** and put your time and energy to better use than spending it all on simply trying to schedule stuff in your life.

Think of **Doodle** as your very own virtual personal secretary, who makes scheduling things in both your personal and professional lives easy and quick. To begin with, start your browser and connect to the **Doodle** app at **http://www.doodle.com** and click on the **Schedule an event** button to start the process of scheduling a meeting.

Doodle and the Doodle logo are registered trademarks of Doodle AG, used with permission.

Doodle and the Doodle logo are registered trademarks of Doodle AG, used with permission.

Enter general information related to the scheduled event (title, location, description and your contact information). Click on the **Next** button to continue.

Enter the proposed dates when you are available to meet the attendees, so that they can choose any date out of the ones you have listed that are convenient for them as well. Click on the **Next** button to continue.

Enter the time slots on the selected dates when you are available, so that the other attendees can choose the slots that are convenient for them as well. This makes the process of choosing a mutually convenient date and time slot extremely easy and hassle-free. Click on the **Next** button to continue.

Doodle and the Doodle logo are registered trademarks of Doodle AG, used with permission.

Now, you can choose to add some optional settings to your **Doodle** meeting scheduler if you want. Click on the **Next** button to continue.

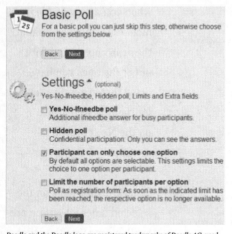

Doodle and the Doodle logo are registered trademarks of Doodle AG, used with permission.

Doodle will create an email link for you, which you can share with your colleagues, clients or friends, so that the most mutually convenient date and time can be selected for your meeting. If you create a free account on **Doodle**, you can also link your Google Calendar and contacts to your **Doodle** account, which will make your scheduling even simpler.

Doodle and the Doodle logo are registered trademarks of Doodle AG, used with permission.

32. HOW TO GOOGLE LIKE A PRO

 < 180 Seconds

If you want to use **Google** faster, better and more precisely than ever before, you can use some simple search tricks, tips and tweaks that only the expert searchers on **Google** know. Most people use **Google** by simply typing in the keywords they want to search for, and then clicking on the search results that are displayed. But there is a lot more to **Google** than just the popularly used keywords-based search function. Depending on what you want to do, it is possible to use **Google Search** shortcuts to quickly access the information that you want.

Google and the Google logo are registered trademarks of Google Inc., used with permission.

1. Unit conversion

If you are measuring your room in preparation for a renovation or want to figure out how cold it really is when your cousin in the US tells you the temperature in Fahrenheit, let **Google** convert various measurement units from one type to another. Unit conversion allows users to convert temperature, length, mass, speed, time, area, volume and others. (Type: 100 inches into cm)

Google and the Google logo are registered trademarks of Google Inc., used with permission.

2. Currency conversion

If you are travelling abroad and want to quickly figure out how much money you need to carry, or if you are paying a vendor abroad and want to figure out how much to send via wire transfer.
(Type: 1000 Japanese Yen into INR)

Google and the Google logo are registered trademarks of Google Inc., used with permission.

3. Flight status

If you are on a business trip and want to find out the gate information for your flight and whether it is on time.
(Type: jetblue 1)

Google and the Google logo are registered trademarks of Google Inc., used with permission.

Google and the Google logo are registered trademarks of Google Inc., used with permission.

Google and the Google logo are registered trademarks of Google Inc., used with permission.

Google and the Google logo are registered trademarks of Google Inc., used with permission.

4.Weather

If you are planning a road trip and want to check the weather forecast for the next few days so that you know what kind of clothes to pack.

(Type: weather shimla)

5. Global time

If you need to a call a relative who lives abroad, or a client in a different time zone.

(Type: time los angeles)

6. Definitions

If you are writing an email to a client or reading an article online and want to find out the exact definition of a particular word. (Type: define:acerbic)

7. Movies

If you want to make weekend plans with your family and want to check which movies are playing in your city and maybe even see their trailers online, **Google** will automatically detect your current location and will look up movies playing in your city. (Type: movie)

Google and the Google logo are registered trademarks of Google Inc., used with permission.

Google and the Google logo are registered trademarks of Google Inc., used with permission.

8. Recipes

If you want to find a particular recipe, simply go to **http://www.google.com/landing/recipes/** and type out of the name of your favourite dish.

(Type: Chicken tikka masala)

9. Specific file types

If you are doing research for a school project or a company presentation and want to find specific file types (for example, PDF or PowerPoint files).

(Type: filetype:pdf newton)

With the help of these simple **Google** search operators, you will be able to enhance your search experience making it faster and easier.

33. HOW TO MANAGE ALL THE TABS IN YOUR BROWSER

 < 60 Seconds

Do you keep multiple tabs open in your browser at the same time and wished there was a better way to manage all of them? **TooManyTabs** is a browser extension that works on both Google Chrome and Mozilla Firefox browsers and allows you to manage all your open tabs efficiently.

Once installed, **TooManyTabs** will add a new button to the URL address bar of your browser. You can click on it any time to view and navigate to any of the open tabs in your browser. You can even search for a specific tab using the **Find** option in the **TooManyTabs** browser app.

Not only that, you can also use **TooManyTabs** to view all the recently closed tabs, to reopen any of the tabs that you may have accidentally closed or that may have closed down due to a software error. Even if the history of your browser is deleted, you can still restore any closed tab using **TooManyTabs**.

Although **TooManyTabs** is available for both Google Chrome and Mozilla Firefox, for Firefox users, I will also recommend the **FoxTab** browser app **(http://www.foxtab.com)** that practically does the same thing, but looks a lot nicer.

34. HOW TO RECOVER FORM DATA IF YOUR COMPUTER CRASHES

 < 120 Seconds

Have you ever spent a long time filling out an online form on some website, and suddenly your computer crashed or froze; and when you went back to that web page, you found that you have lost all the data that you had spent so much time typing? Have you ever been in a situation where, after you submitted an online form, you were shown an error message and when you hit the back button, all your form data was lost? Such situations can not only leave you frustrated, they will also waste your time, since you will have to fill out the entire form again.

For exactly such situations (network errors, crashes, frozen browsers and others), there is a very useful browser extension called **Lazarus (www.getlazarus.com)**, available for both Google Chrome and Mozilla Firefox browsers. This browser app will automatically save all the data that you type into any online form in your browser and will allow you to recover this saved data in case it is required.

Once you have installed **Lazarus** on your computer, the next time you are filling out any field in a form on a website, you will notice a small icon on the extreme right end of the input field. This signifies that **Lazarus** is running in the background and automatically saving everything that you are typing into the form.

Let us assume that, while filling out this online form, suddenly your computer crashes or there is a network error and you lose your form. In such a scenario, you can reopen your browser to the same form and click on the **Lazarus** icon in the input fields to recover the form data that was automatically saved by **Lazarus**.

If you are worried that somebody else using your computer will be able to misuse your private data saved in **Lazarus**, it is possible to enable security in such a way that you will be asked to enter a password to recover the saved form data from **Lazarus**. You can also disable **Lazarus** on certain websites from which you don't want it to record any form data. All these options can be accessed by clicking on the **Lazarus** icon on the input field of a form, and then clicking **Lazarus Options**.

With **Lazarus** in your browser, you will never need to worry about losing any form data due to a network error or computer crash.

35. HOW TO INCREASE YOUR COMPUTER'S SPEED

 < 300 Seconds

All of us are constantly striving for increased personal productivity. It is obvious that the faster the processer and greater the RAM, the faster your computer will run. Here are some simple tips that can be implemented on your computer to increase its speed.

Disk Cleanup and the Disk Cleanup logo are registered trademarks of the Microsoft Corporation, used with permission.

1. Disk Cleanup

All Windows systems come with the **Disk Cleanup** tool preinstalled. It can be accessed via the quick search option in the Start menu. **Disk Cleanup** will search your entire hard drive and tell you which files can be safely deleted to free up some space on your hard drive. The more space you free up, the faster your computer will run. It is recommended that you run **Disk Cleanup** every fifteen days or so, in order to keep your computer running at optimum speed.

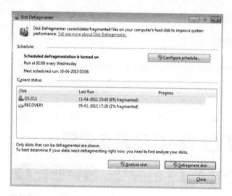

2. Disk Defragmenter
Another tool that comes preinstalled with Windows is **Disk Defragmenter**. Over a period of time, data on your hard drive gets fragmented, which makes your hard drive do extra work that slows down

Disk Cleanup and the Disk Cleanup logo are registered trademarks of the Microsoft Corporation, used with permission.

your computer. The **Disk Defragmenter** tool will defragment data on your hard drive, making your computer run faster. The **Disk Defragmenter** tool can be accessed through the Start menu. Microsoft recommends it is a good idea to run the tool whenever your hard drive is fragmented by more than 10 per cent.

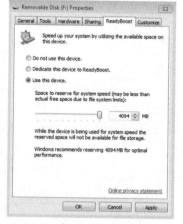

Disk Cleanup and the Disk Cleanup logo are registered trademarks of the Microsoft Corporation, used with permission.

3. ReadyBoost
Readyboost is an option in Windows that allows you to use the

memory of a USB flash drive, SD card or any portable flash memory card as cache memory to boost your system performance. As soon as you plug in a pen drive or SD card to your computer, the **AutoPlay** options should show up on the screen in which there will be an option to **Speed up my System Using Windows ReadyBoost**. Select this option and follow the instructions on the screen to enable **ReadyBoost**. Now your computer will start using the extra memory from your external drive to boost its speed and performance.

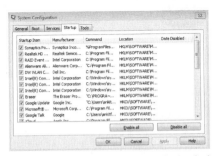

Disk Cleanup and the Disk Cleanup logo are registered trademarks of the Microsoft Corporation, used with permission.

4. MSCONFIG

Whenever you start Windows, there are numerous apps that automatically get loaded into the memory, occupying valuable system resources. It is important to run the **MSCONFIG** tool (accessible from the Start menu) periodically to check which apps are automatically starting with Windows. It is advisable to disable all non-crucial apps that you don't actually require or use, in order to free up some memory on your computer. This will significantly improve not only the general speed of your computer but also the amount of time it takes for your computer to start.

5. Disable Search Indexing

The latest versions of Windows use something known as **Search Indexing** to index your entire hard drive and help you search better and faster. However, **Search Indexing** has a slowing-down effect on your computer. If you wish to disable **Search Indexing**

on your computer, simply go to **My Computer** > Right-click on
C: and select **Properties**. Under the **General** tab there will be an
option to disable **Search Indexing**.

*Disk Cleanup and the Disk Cleanup logo
are registered trademarks of the Microsoft
Corporation, used with permission.*

36. HOW TO BLOCK ADS ON WEBSITES

 < 120 Seconds

Let's admit it, no one likes ads. They are a waste of time, slow down
your browsing experience, clog up valuable bandwidth and clutter
up web pages. However, the good news is that it is possible for you
to block ads from being displayed on your favourite websites with
the help of the **Adblock Plus** browser extension. It is available as a
free download from **http://adblockplus.org** and can be installed
on most popular browsers.

Adblock Plus and the Adblock Plus logo are registered trademarks of Eyeo GmbH, used with permission.

Once installed, **Adblock Plus** will automatically block all ads on websites you visit and prevent them from getting displayed on your screen, including the following:

1. Google ads in search results

2. YouTube video ads at the start of a video

3. Facebook ads

4 .Banner ads

5. Pop-up ads

Moreover, with **AdBlock Plus** it is very easy for you to toggle between enabling and disabling ads on a particular website based on your personal preferences, by simply clicking on the **AdBlock Plus** icon in your URL address bar. Not that there will be too many occasions when you want to enable ads on a website!

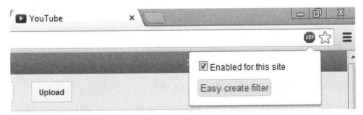

Adblock Plus and the Adblock Plus logo are registered trademarks of Eyeo GmbH, used with permission.

With **AdBlock Plus** in your browser, you will never need to worry about being bombarded with annoying ads on your favourite websites and instead will be able to enjoy an ad-free browsing experience.

37. HOW TO UPDATE YOUR FACEBOOK STATUS OR TWEET IN THE FUTURE

 < 60 Seconds

Have you ever wanted to update your Facebook status at a future time and date when you may not actually have the time to do it? Have you ever wanted to tweet something in the future, but type it out now in the present? Perhaps send out a reminder for an upcoming event that you are organizing or managing?

Postcron is a web-based free app that allows you to schedule Facebook status messages and Twitter tweets at the predefined time and date in the future.

To use this app start your browser and connect to **Postcron (http://www.postcron.com)** and sign in to your Facebook account.

You will need to select the time zone that you are in, so that **Postcron** can accurately update your Facebook status in the future at a predefined time and date specified by you.

Once you have connected the **Postcron** app to your Facebook account, you can specify what message you wish to post on your Facebook account and at what future time and date. Click on **Schedule** and let **Postcron** do the rest. Not only can you schedule plain text updates in the future, you can use **Postcron** to send out updates with photos and links as well.

Postcron and the Postcron logo are registered trademarks of Postcron Inc., used with permission.

You can also connect **Postcron** to your Twitter account and Facebook pages that you manage and send out updates or messages in the future.

Several other apps allow you update your social networking accounts in the future. Some of them are:

▶ **Hootsuite (http://hootsuite.com)**

▶ **LaterBro (http://laterbro.com)**

▶ **TweetDeck (http://tweetdeck.com)**

▶ **Social Tomorrow (http://socialtomorrow.com)**

38. HOW TO SAVE MONEY ON YOUR MOBILE PHONE DATA PLANS

 < 60 Seconds

Do you want to save money on your mobile phone data plans and get more data on your phone at the same price? Normally, whenever you need details about your phone data usage, you either have to guess or rely on the usage trackers provided by your mobile phone provider, which may not be completely reliable. This leads to unexpectedly exorbitant bills.

Onavo Count and the Onavo Count logo are registered trademarks of Onavo Mobile Ltd, used with permission.

You can stop guessing your phone data usage and put an end to exorbitant bills by getting the **Onavo Count** app on your phone. It is available as a free download for both the Android and the iPhone platforms. Once installed on your phone, **Onavo Count** will tell you how much data has been used on your phone by each app segregated by 2G/3G/4G/LTE, so that you can monitor, tweak and control your data usage.

It is also possible for you to extend your data plan by installing the **Onavo Extend** app on your phone (also available for free for both Android and iPhone devices). Once installed on your phone, it will compress your data usage by up to 500 per cent, hence allowing you to get five times the data at the same price.

Onavo Extend and the Onavo Extend logo are registered trademarks of Onavo Mobile Ltd, used with permission.

39. HOW TO ORGANIZE, SEARCH, MANAGE AND SHARE YOUR PICTURES EASILY

 < 300 Seconds

Nowadays, taking photos has become extremely easy with high-quality cameras built into smartphones and tablets. The popularity of social networking websites has made it even more compelling for people to capture even mundane aspects of their daily life using pictures.

However, a common problem that many people face is how to store, organize, edit, share and publish all their photos in an easy manner. The answer to all your photo-related problems lies in the wonderful free **Picasa** software from Google, which is available as a free download from **http://picasa.google.com**. In classic Google style, **Picasa** does a fantastic job of automatically searching, importing and organizing all your photos and videos from various sources on your hard drive and the Internet into different albums. These albums are then automatically classified by **Picasa** based on their year, folder name, import source (the Internet or local hard drive), geographical location and also by the people in the pictures. This makes it very simple for you to search for specific photos using **Picasa**.

Picasa also makes sharing your photos and videos a breeze by seamlessly allowing you to upload your photos to a web album (which can be shared with the public or specific people), publish them on a blog or just email them directly to friends.

Picasa also makes it very easy for users to do the basic editing, cropping and retouching of photos from within the app itself. What makes editing fun with **Picasa** are its various image-processing options. They can really help you make your photos a lot of fun and perhaps even more professional. Try the **Pencil Sketch, Cinemascope, HDR-ish, Cross Process** and **Focal Zoom** options for some very cool-looking pictures.

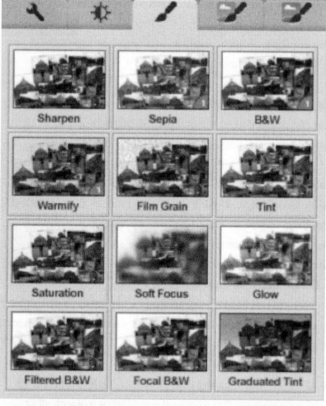

Picasa and the Picasa logo are registered trademarks of Google Inc., used with permission.

If you travel quite a bit or simply want to show off your exotic travel adventures to your friends, you can even use **Picasa** to **Geotag** your pictures on Google Earth. Simply select all the

Picasa and the Picasa logo are registered trademarks of Google Inc., used with permission.

photos you wish to **Geotag** in the **Picasa** app.

Click on **Tools > Geotag> Geotag with Google Earth** and this will open the Google Earth app. To **Geotag** your pictures, simply navigate the entire world to the location where you took the photos, position the crosshairs icon and then click on the **Geotag** button.

Picasa and the Picasa logo are registered trademarks of Google Inc., used with permission.
Google Earth and the Google Earth logo are registered trademarks of Google Inc., used with permission.

Now you can share these photos with your friends with the relevant geographical location **Geotags** visible!

One of my favourite features in **Picasa** is the **Picture Collage**

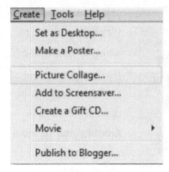

feature that allows you to create a collage out of a bunch of selected photos in a matter of a few seconds. If you just came back from a memorable vacation and want to create a collage out of all your favourite photos or if it's a special occasion and you want to surprise a loved one by creating a collage of some special photos, then in simply select the photos that you would like to use in **Picasa** and click on **Create** > **Picture Collage**.

The best part is that **Picasa** gives you lots of options and ways to completely customize the collage based on your personal preferences. It is also possible for you to individually click on any photo in the collage to change its position, angle and size. Moreover, if you don't like the overall shape of the collage or the positioning of photos within the collage, you can make use of the **Scramble Collage** and **Shuffle Pictures** button below the pictures.

Scramble Collage	Shuffle Pictures	View and Edit

Using the left column in the **Picture Collage** feature of **Picasa**, it is possible to further customize the collage to suit your personal preferences and requirements.

You can click on the **Page Format** drop-down menu to change the size of the collage to any size of your choice depending upon where you plan to use it.

Picasa and the Picasa logo are registered trademarks of Google Inc., used with permission.

You can also choose from a range of styles (**Mosaic, Frame Mosaic, Grid** and others).

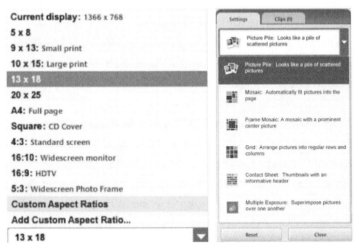

Picasa and the Picasa logo are registered trademarks of Google Inc., used with permission.

Once you are happy with the style, size and look of the collage that you have created, you simply need to click on the **Create Collage** button in the left column for it to be processed.

Picasa and the Picasa logo are registered trademarks of Google Inc., used with permission.

The best feature in **Picasa** is called **Face Detection**, which has built-in intelligence to scan through your complete photo collection and detect faces of all your friends and identify them by their names! Whenever **Picasa** detects a new face for the first time or finds a face it can't recognize, it will ask you to give a new name to it. Once you have given a name to a new face that was found, **Picasa** will automatically search the rest of the photos and recognize other photos of that same person. No need to individually open each photo and tag your friends one by one. Once **Picasa** has tagged photos of a particular person or face, it also allows you to use the search feature to search for photos of your friends and family members by name. The only thing that **Picasa** can't do, unfortunately, is make us look prettier and nicer!

A very cool experimental feature in **Picasa** is the **Passport Photo** functionality that allows you to convert absolutely any photo of your choice into a passport-sized photo with a single click of the mouse button. Most countries require the dimensions of a passport-sized photo to be approximately 2 x 2 inches or 35 x 45 mm. All you need is a good high-quality colour printer and even you can start creating your own passport photos at home with the help of **Picasa**.

To create a passport photo, all you need to do is to select the photo of your choice that you want to convert into a passport photo. Click on **Tools** > **Experimental** > **Passport Photo** and, within a few seconds, **Picasa** will convert the selected picture into a passport-sized photo, all ready to be printed immediately with an attached printer. If you are not too happy about how the passport photo was framed by **Picasa** by default, you can crop the photo according to your needs before processing it with the **Passport Photo** feature.

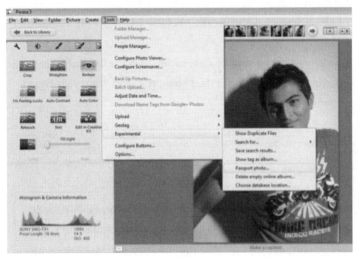

Picasa and the Picasa logo are registered trademarks of Google Inc., used with permission.

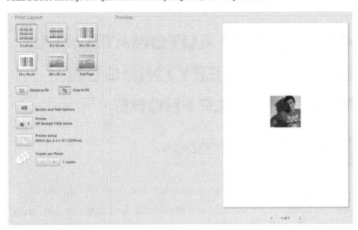

Picasa and the Picasa logo are registered trademarks of Google Inc., used with permission.

If you are a heavy **Picasa** user, it probably will make sense to further integrate **Picasa** with your Gmail account. There is a useful Gmail Labs feature called **Picasa previews in mail**, which, like the name suggests, shows you photo previews within Gmail whenever you receive a **Picasa** photo album link from any of your friends. To enable this feature, simply log in to your Gmail account and click on **Settings** > **Labs** > Scroll down to **Picasa preview in mail** > Click **Enable**.

Now whenever you receive a photo album in the form of a **Picasa** link, you will be able to see the photo previews within your Gmail account itself.

Picasa and the Picasa logo are registered trademarks of Google Inc., used with permission.

It is also possible for you to download the **Picasa** mobile app to your smartphone so that you can manage, view and share your photos with your friends from your Android or iOS device.

40. HOW TO AUTOMATICALLY BACK UP EVERYTHING ON YOUR MOBILE PHONE

 < 300 Seconds

If your mobile phone ever goes missing, won't you be relieved if you had backed up your data at a secure place so that you can easily restore it? I recommend that all mobile phone users back up all their data on a regular basis.

The Google Backup and Restore feature is a registered trademark of Google Inc., used with permission.

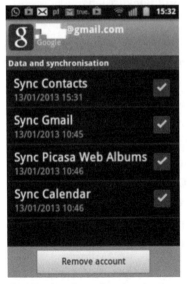

The Google Backup and Restore feature is a registered trademark of Google Inc., used with permission.

If you use Android, Google allows you to automatically back up all your apps and device settings data to your Google account, so that in case you ever have to change your device, you can easily restore your lost data. The **Google Backup and Restore** service allows you to back up your device settings and application data like your contacts, calendar, apps that you installed from your Google Play account, browser bookmarks, user dictionary, Wi-Fi passwords and other data. All this data is backed up and securely stored on the Google server and can be easily restored whenever required. To enable automatic back-up and restoration on your Android phone, go to **Settings** > **Privacy** and enable the **Back up my data** and **Automatic restore** options.

Next go to **Settings** > **Accounts and sync** > Select your Gmail Account > Select all the things that you wish to back up. The **Google Backup and Restore** feature is now set up on your mobile phone and in case you ever need to change your mobile device, then you simply need to log in to the same Gmail account using your new device and you will be able to easily restore all your backed up data.

Although Google's built-in **Backup and Restore** feature is quite useful, it comes with its own limitations. It does not back up your valuable SMS messages and call logs. If you want to back up all the

The Google Backup and Restore feature is a registered trademark of Google Inc., used with permission.

SMS text messages and call logs from your Android phone, then I recommend that you use the **G Cloud Backup** app.

It is one of the best apps for effortlessly backing up just about everything from your Android phone (photos, videos, messages, call logs, browser data, documents, device settings etc.) to a secure cloud so that you never lose any of it. The **G Cloud Backup** app is available as a free download from the Google Play App Store and gives you 1 GB of free storage space where you can back up data from your Android phone.

G Cloud Backup and the G Cloud Backup logo are registered trademarks of the Genie9 Corporation, used with permission.

Once you launch **G Cloud Backup** on your Android phone, it will

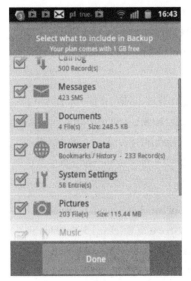

ask you to create an account.

Once you have created an account, **G Cloud Backup** will ask you to choose data from your phone that you wish to safely back up on its secure cloud. Press the **Done** button when you have finished selecting the items you wish to back up.

G Cloud Backup and the G Cloud Backup logo are registered trademarks of the Genie9 Corporation, used with permission.

G Cloud Backup will now automatically back up all the selected data from your Android phone to its secure cloud on a regular basis. You can press the **Settings** button to choose various settings related to the back-up process. For example, you can schedule the back-up at specific times or you can specify that the back-up should only happen when your phone is connected on Wi-Fi.

G Cloud Backup and the G Cloud Backup logo are registered trademarks of the Genie9 Corporation, used with permission.

In case you lose your phone or switch to a new phone and want to restore your data, simply install **G Cloud Backup** app and press the **Existing User/Restore** button and you will be able to restore all the backed-up data.

On the other hand, if you are using an iOS device, it is easy to configure your device to automatically back up all the important data to Apple's **iCloud** storage space. By default, every user gets 5 GB of free storage space on the **iCloud**. In case that is not enough, you can always purchase more storage space.

To enable automatic back-up to the **iCloud** on your iOS device, simply press **Settings** > **iCloud** > **Store & Backup** > Enable the **iCloud Backup** option. Once you enable this option, all your contacts, photos, email, documents, device settings and accounts will be automatically backed up to the **iCloud** whenever your iOS device is plugged in, locked and connected to Wi-Fi. To choose what data from your iOS device gets automatically backed up to your **iCloud**, go to **Settings** > **iCloud** and in the right pane select all the data you want to back up. Once you have enabled the back-up to the **iCloud** feature, even if you lose your device or switch to a new device, you can easily restore all your backed-up data from the cloud.

In case your Wi-Fi access is slow and you have a lot of data to back up, it is also possible for you to back up all the important data from your iOS device to your computer using **iTunes**. Connect your iOS device to your computer using the USB cable and in the left pane of **iTunes**, under devices, right-click on your device and select **Backup** and your data will be backed up on your computer.

To restore your backed-up data, connect your new device to your computer and, inside **iTunes**, right-click on the device and select the **Restore from Backup** option.

41. HOW TO SEND CANNED RESPONSES TO EMAILS AUTOMATICALLY

 < 60 Seconds

There are so many situations in our professional and personal lives in which we are required to send an email with the same text to different people. Normally, we have to type these standard emails over and over again, which is a colossal waste of time. A trick that many people use is to save a set of standard replies in a Notepad file and then manually copy-paste them into emails before sending them out. However, that too is quite inefficient. This is where a Gmail Labs feature called **Canned responses** can be a time-saver.

Canned responses is a Gmail Labs feature that allows users to save commonly used replies and include them in an email easily and quickly right from the **Compose** page in Gmail.

To enable the **Canned responses** feature in your Gmail account, click on **Settings** > **Labs** > Scroll down to the **Canned reponses** feature and select **Enable** > Scroll down and click on **Save changes**.

Insert	**Canned Responses**	⦿ Enable
Refer to documentation	by Chad P	⊙ Disable
Status report template	Email for the truly lazy. Save and then send your common	Send feedback
FAQ	messages using a button next to the compose form. Also automatically send emails using filters.	

Canned Responses is the registered trademark of Google Inc., used with permission.

Once you have enabled the **Canned responses** option, to save a message as a **Canned response**, click on **Compose** and type any message of your choice in the body of the email. I am going to create a **Canned response** containing an address: 500 Park Ave, New York City, NY 10022, Between 58th St and 59th St.

Canned Responses is the registered trademark of Google Inc., used with permission.

Now click on the **Canned responses** link > **New canned response** and then choose any name under which you wish to save the **Canned response** and click on the **OK** button. I have used 'Address' as the name of this **Canned response**.

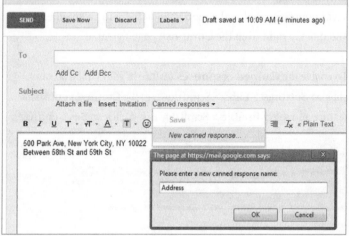

Canned Responses is the registered trademark of Google Inc., used with permission.

Now the **Canned response** has been saved and is ready for use in any future emails that you send out. Whenever I need to send my address to someone, I can click on the **Canned responses** link in the **Compose** screen and under **Insert** select the name of the **Canned response** you wish to use. In this case, I have selected the 'Address' Canned Response. Within a few seconds, you will notice the saved **Canned response** has been inserted into the email.

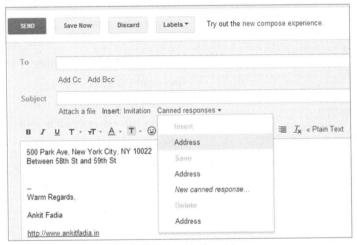

Canned Responses is a registered trademark of Google Inc., used with permission.

This process can also be automated by creating filters in your Gmail account. Filters are rules that are defined so that Gmail will search all incoming email for certain characteristics (sender, subject, key words in the message etc.) and, whenever a match is found, it will perform some action on it.

To create a filtering rule, open the message based on which you want to create the rule, click on the **More** button and then click on the **Filter messages like these** option.

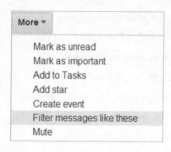

Canned Responses is a registered trademark of Google Inc., used with permission.

Gmail will automatically analyse the open email and create a filter based on the sender's email address. You may modify the filter based on your requirements. Once you have created the filter rules, simply click on the **Create filter with this search** option at the bottom right corner.

Gmail will now ask you what you would like to do when email messages matching the filtering rule are received in your inbox. In this case, you want to automatically send a **Canned response** to all messages matching the predefined filtering rules. So you need to first select the **Send canned response** option and then select the specific canned message you want to send as a reply and then click on the **Create filter** button.

Canned Responses is a registered trademark of Google Inc., used with permission.

42. HOW TO HIDE FILES INSIDE PHOTOGRAPHS

 < 120 Seconds

Sometimes hiding data is as much about encryption and password-protection as it is about managing appearances. In this tip we are going to see how easy it is for you to take all your confidential files and hide them inside photos (or even music or video files).

In other words, if someone were to go through the files on your computer then they will only see regular photos. However, little do they realize that inside these photos actually lies your confidential data.

The technique of hiding files or data inside photos, songs and videos is known as Steganography. One of my favourite Steganography tools is **S-Tools** which is available as a free download.

First you need to identify the confidential file that you wish to hide and the photo inside which you wish to hide it. Ideally, if the size of the confidential file is large, the photo that you choose should be appropriately large in size as well. Or you can also move from using a photo to a song and finally to using a video. In the following example, I am going to hide a Notepad file containing my bank account details (account number, username and password) inside the photo of a cute baby.

Bank Name: ABC Bank.
City: Zurich, Switzerland
Account Number: 550 870 0192 0191 9015
Username: ankitfadia
Password: ankit123!&

S-Tools and the S-Tools logo are registered trademarks of SpyChecker.com, used with permission.

S-Tools and the S-Tools logo are registered trademarks of SpyChecker.com, used with permission.

Start the **S-Tools** software on your computer and drag the photo on to the software tab. The photo will now appear inside the **S-Tools** software. In the bottom right corner of the screen, **S-Tools** will tell you how much data can be hidden inside this particular photo. In this case, the selected photo can hold up to 29,387 bytes.

Drag and drop the file you wish to hide on to the photo inside the **S-Tools** software. You will be asked to choose a password to protect your hidden data. Enter any password of your choice and click on the **OK** button to continue.

Within a few seconds, **S-Tools** will create an identical copy of the photo and will display it on the screen. By just looking at the two photos, the human eye will not be able to differentiate between them. The only difference is that the photo on the left does

S-Tools and the S-Tools logo are registered trademarks of SpyChecker.com, used with permission.

not contain any hidden data (you can close that image) and the photo on the right contains the confidential file hidden inside.

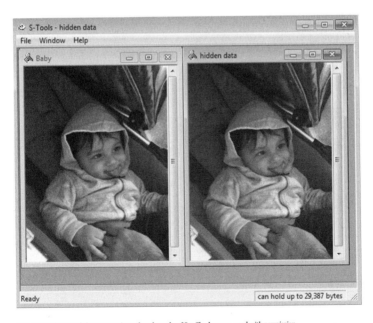

S-Tools and the S-Tools logo are registered trademarks of SpyChecker.com, used with permission.

Right-click on the photo and save it with any file name of your choice anywhere on your system.

S-Tools and the S-Tools logo are registered trademarks of SpyChecker.com., used with permission.

If someone were to access your computer and open the above photo, it will look quite normal and will not show any tangible signs of any hidden data embedded inside. It is important to note that the size of the photo may change slightly, depending on the size of the file you are hiding. However, since there is no way for someone to know the original file size of the photo, the change in file size isn't a giveaway.

To retrieve and reveal the hidden file from inside the photo all you need to do is follow the steps below:

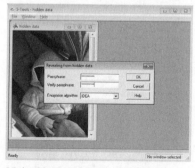

S-Tools and the S-Tools logo are registered trademarks of SpyChecker.com, used with permission.

Start the **S-Tools** software and drag on to it the photo containing the hidden data. Right-click on the photo and select the **Reveal** option.

Enter the same password that you had entered while hiding the data and click on the **OK** button to reveal the hidden confidential files.

Within a few seconds, **S-Tools** will retrieve the hidden file from inside the photo and reveal it on the screen. Right-click on the revealed file and save it anywhere on your computer to view it.

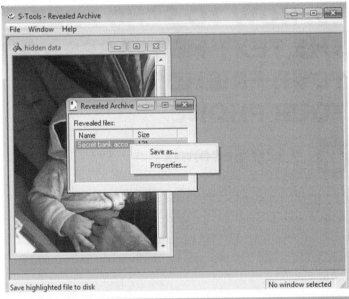

S-Tools and the S-Tools logo are registered trademarks of SpyChecker.com, used with permission.

To further increase your security, I would recommend combining the Steganography technique with the password-protection and encryption techniques that I have discussed later in this book.

Sometimes, concealing in plain sight is the best place to hide.

43. HOW TO SEND FREE SMS TEXT MESSAGES TO YOUR FRIENDS FROM YOUR PHONE

 < 120 Seconds

Do you wish you could send free text messages from your mobile phone to your friends? Are you tired of paying for sending text messages to your friends? Put an end to your SMS texting bills and start sending SMS text messages for free by using the **Free SMS India** app.

You can download the **Free SMS India** app absolutely free of cost from the Google Play App Store to your Android phone. Once installed, it allows you send free SMS messages from your Android phone using the Internet data plan on your phone! The SMS text messages get delivered to the recipient as a regular SMS, since they are routed by the app through popular free SMS gateways. By using this app, you no longer need to pay for sending SMS text messages. The **Free SMS India** app supports the following free SMS gateways:

- www.Way2SMS.com
- www.FullonSMS.com
- www.Site2SMS.com
- www.16oby2.com
- www.YouMint.com
- www.IndyaRocks.com

▶ **www.SMS440.com**

▶ **www.ultoo.com**

▶ **www.freeSMS8.in**

The way these SMS gateways are able to allow you to send free text messages is by sending you email and SMS ads. But if you do not mind viewing a few ads, **Free SMS India** is perfect for you.

Before you can start using **Free SMS India**, you need to create an account for free with any of the SMS gateways that it supports. Typically, most SMS gateways put a restriction on the number of free SMS messages you will be allowed to send per day; however, that limit is adequate enough for most users. For example, the **Way2SMS.com** SMS gateway allows you to send a hundred free SMS messages per day. If you are an SMS addict and this daily limit is not enough for you, simply create another account with some other SMS gateway supported by the **Free SMS India** app!

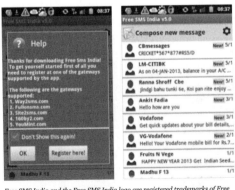

Now start the **Free SMS India** app on your Android phone. It will display all the messages that you have in your SMS message inbox within its interface. You can read, reply and

Free SMS India and the Free SMS India logo are registered trademarks of Free SMS India, used with permission.

send messages just the way you normally do, except that you no longer need to pay for sending messages.

Before you can start sending free messages using **Free SMS India**, you need to choose the SMS gateway you want to use. Go to **Preference** > **Setup Gateways** > Choose any SMS gateway of your choice from the list. I am going to select the **Way2SMS** gateway in this example.

Free SMS India and the Free SMS India logo are registered trademarks of Free SMS India, used with permission.

Select the **Enter Login Details** option and enter the log-in details of your SMS gateway account (**Way2SMS** in this case).

Free SMS India and the Free SMS India logo are registered trademarks of Free SMS India, used with permission.

You can configure a default SMS gateway for sending free SMS text messages by going to **Preference** > **Select Default Gateway**.

Free SMS India is now configured on your Android phone to send free SMS text messages via the SMS gateway of your choice. If you reach the daily SMS limit for your SMS gateway, simply switch to another gateway. Enjoy!

Free SMS India and the Free SMS India logo are registered trademarks of Free SMS India, used with permission.

With the help of the **Free SMS India** app, you don't need to worry about paying for sending SMS text messages from your mobile phone ever again!

44. HOW TO TURN YOUR PHONE INTO A FLASHLIGHT

 < 60 Seconds

If you are walking back home at night on an unlit street or trying to make your way up your apartment stairway in the dark, or if you are trying to get to your seats in a dark movie theatre hall, then most of us tend to unlock our mobile phones to use its screen light to see better. A more effective option is to use a flashlight app that will help you see things in the dark by turning your mobile phone into a flashlight, as though you were holding a torch.

Depending upon the device and platform you are using, flashlight apps will help you see better by either turning on the camera flash function on your phone or by turning your screen brightness to maximum. If you are trying to get someone's attention, some apps will also allow you to make use of the blinking mode on your phone, mimicking a flashlight that is being continuously switched on and off.

iOS users can download the **Flashlight** app by Surpax Technology from the iTunes app store and Android users can download the **Flashlight** app by Intellectual Flame from the Google Play App Store. With the **Flashlight** app on your phone, you can see well even in the dark.

45. HOW TO CREATE A PERSONAL WI-FI HOTSPOT USING YOUR MOBILE PHONE

 < 60 Seconds

Android and the Android logo are registered trademarks of Google Inc., used with permission.

Android and the Android logo are registered trademarks of Google Inc., used with permission.

If you have a mobile phone with a data plan on it, it is possible to create a personal Wi-Fi hotspot around you, anywhere at any time so that you can get Internet access on your laptop and other Wi-Fi devices. To create a personal Wi-Fi hotspot using your Internet enabled Android mobile phone, simply follow the steps below:

Go to **Settings** > **Wireless and Networks** and then press the **Tethering and Portable Hotspot** option.

Enable the **Portable Wi-Fi hotspot** option. If you notice, in the screenshot on the left, my phone has displayed a message that the Portable Wi-Fi Hotspot AndroidAP9981 is active.

You can change the name of your Wi-Fi hotspot, password-protect it and manage all its settings by pressing the **Portable Wi-Fi Hotspot Settings** option and entering the necessary details. For example, in the example below, I've named my Wi-Fi hotspot 'Ankit Fadia Android', enabled WPA2 security on it and also put an access password on it so that unauthorized users will not be able to connect to it. Press the **Save** button and the Wi-Hi hotspot will be ready for use.

You can now use any Wi-Fi-enabled device to connect to the Internet using the Wi-Fi hotspot created using your Android phone.

Similarly, you can create your very own personal hotspot using an iPhone with an Internet data plan.

Android and the Android logo are registered trademarks of Google Inc., used with permission.

On the home screen of your iPhone or iPad, press **Settings** and then press **Personal Hotspot** to enable it. In case you don't find the **Personal Hotspot** option, go to **Settings** > **General** > **Cellular Data** > **Personal Hotspot** and enable it.

Turn on the **Personal Hotspot** option.

You will be given the option to enable the **Personal Hotspot** either over only Bluetooth and USB or over Wi-Fi as well. Select the **Turn on Wi-Fi** option.

Choose any Wi-Fi password from the **Wi-Fi Password** option. You are now ready to access the Internet using the data plan on your iPhone or iPad, or using any other Wi-Fi-enabled device, like your laptop.

Using this technique, you can use the Internet access on your mobile phone to create a personal Wi-fi hotspot wherever you go and connect all your devices to the Internet.

46. HOW TO RECORD AND SHARE YOUR MOVEMENTS OUTDOORS

 < 120 Seconds

Have you ever gone on a trek and wished there was a way for you to record and track your movements using GPS so that you can trace your route back? Do you go out running or biking and want to record your vital stats (path, speed, distance and elevation)? Are you planning a road trip and want to record the vital stats of your trip? Google's **My Tracks** is an Android app available as a free download from the Google Play App Store that allows you to do all of that and more.

Once installed on your Android phone, simply start the **My Tracks** app and press the **Record** button to start recording your path, movements and vital stats. **My Tracks** will use the GPS feature on your mobile phone to track your location and data access to plot your location on Google Maps. You can safely put your phone in your pocket while it continues to record all your movements. Press the **Stop** button whenever you are done.

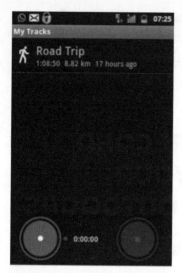 

My Tracks and the My Tracks logo are registered trademarks of Google Inc., used with permission.

The **My Tracks** app will record all your movements and plot your path on a Google Map on the screen, so that you always know your current location and can easily find your way back if you are lost.

My Tracks and the My Tracks logo are registered trademarks of Google Inc., used with permission.

My Tracks will also record all your vital stats, so that you know how far you have gone and how fast you travelled.

 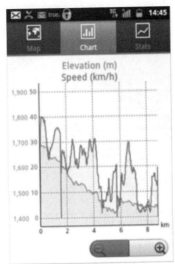

My Tracks and the My Tracks logo are registered trademarks of Google Inc., used with permission.

47. HOW TO MEASURE EVERYTHING USING YOUR MOBILE PHONE

 < 180 Seconds

Have you ever wanted to measure the distance, height, length, width, angle and sound of things, people and places around you, but did not have the measurement tools with you? Don't worry, with the **Smart Tools** app, the only measurement tool that you will ever need is going to be your mobile phone.

Smart Tools is an Android app that is available in the Google Play App Store. Once downloaded on your phone, it will allow you to measure just about anything right from your Android phone. For iPhone users, **Multi Measures** is a good alternative app that I would like to recommend.

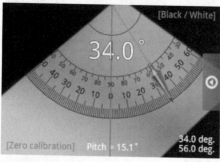

1. Length and Angle

If there are any small objects whose length or angle you wish to measure, you can the **Smart Tools** app's built-in ruler and protractor.

Smart Tools and the Smart Tools app are registered trademarks of Smart Tools, used with permission.

2. Distance, Height, Width and Area

One of the best features in the **Smart Tools** app is its almost magical distance and height measurement feature. It allows you to measure the distance and height of people, landmarks, objects and places. Imagine that you doing up your house and need to measure some lengths and heights. You can now do that just using your Android phone!

Once you have started the **Distance** tool in the **Smart Tools** app, to measure the distance between you and a particular object, point the crosshair

Smart Tools and the Smart Tools app are registered trademarks of Smart Tools, used with permission.

icon to the bottom of the object and press the **Shutter** button. In this example, the distance between you and the object is 1.7 metres.

To measure the height of the object (the piece of furniture to which we recorded the distance in the previous example), press the height button on the left.

Smart Tools and the Smart Tools app are registered trademarks of Smart Tools, used with permission.

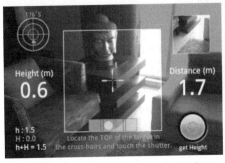

Starting at the bottom of the object, move the mobile phone to point where the crosshair icon reaches the top of the object. Press the **Shutter** button on the bottom right corner of the screen

Smart Tools and the Smart Tools app are registered trademarks of Smart Tools, used with permission.

to record the height of the object. For example, in this case the height of the furniture is 0.6 metres.

Smart Tools and the Smart Tools app are registered trademarks of Smart Tools, used with permission.

For more accurate measurements, you can change the height of the mobile phone from the ground from the default value of 1.5 metres. Basic understanding of trigonometry will also be helpful in ensuring that your measurements are accurate. To calculate the width and area of a particular object or place, press the **Settings** button on your phone and change what you wish to measure.

Smart Tools and the Smart Tools app are registered trademarks of Smart Tools, used with permission.

3. Compass

The **Compass** tool will convert your Android phone into a conventional magnetic compass. It displays your current GPS location coordinates and a compass so that you know in which direction you are going.

Smart Tools and the Smart Tools app are registered trademarks of Smart Tools, used with permission.

4. Metal Detector

Most smartphones come with a magnetic sensor built in. The **Metal Detector** feature of the **Smart Tools** app converts your mobile phone into a metal detector (like the ones found at the security queue at airports) and allows you to find any metalic object around you. Once you start the **Metal Detector** feature, the measured magnetic field is displayed on the screen. Whenever the magnetic field is within normal levels, you will see the green bar. If the magnetic field value exceeds normal levels, the red bar will be displayed on the screen and it means that you have detected metal.

5. Sound and Vibration Meters

This feature allows you to record the sound and vibration levels around you!

48. HOW TO TAKE PROFESSIONAL PHOTOS WITH YOUR MOBILE PHONE

< 120 Seconds

If you have ever wished you could take professional-looking photos directly from your mobile phone, you will love the **Camera Zoom FX** app.

It is available for only Rs 150 from the Google Play App Store and is my favourite photo app for the Android platform. Once you have installed the **Camera Zoom FX** app on your Android phone, you can make use of a variety of shooting modes that include:

1. Stable Shot
This feature will wait until your phone is stable and only then will it take the picture; you can say goodbye to blurry pictures. There is also an on-screen meter that tells you how stable
the phone is at present.

2. Voice Activated
Allows you to take a picture by making a loud noise or clap. This feature is perfect for group photos!

3. Burst Mode
Takes up to 10 shots per second, allowing you to take fantastic shots of moving objects, people and things.

4. Time Lapse

Allows you to take multiple pictures with a time lapse in between.

Camera Zoom FX and the Camera Zoom FX logo are registered trademarks of Camera Zoom FX 2012, used with permission.

In addition to all of this, **Camera Zoom FX** comes with all the special effects and editing tools that are normally found in a professional photo-editing software—standard photo-editing, special effects, mirror effects, distortion, tilting, cropping, collage and many others.

For iOS users, a good alternate app that I would like to recommend is the **SnapSeed** app.

49. HOW TO SEND AN SMS TEXT MESSAGE IN THE FUTURE

 < 60 Seconds

We have already seen how useful it can be to be able to schedule an email, tweet or Facebook status update to be sent in the future. Wouldn't it be great if it were possible for you to even send an SMS text message from your mobile phone in the future? **SMS Scheduler** is a free app available from the Google Play App Store for Android devices that allows you to do exactly that.

Start the **SMS Scheduler** app on your Android phone and click on the **Add** button to schedule an SMS text message to be sent at a predefined date and time in the future.

SMS Scheduler and the SMS Scheduler logo are registered trademarks of SMS Scheduler, used with permission.

SMS Scheduler and the SMS Scheduler logo are registered trademarks of SMS Scheduler, used with permission.

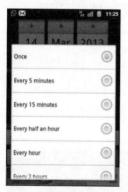

SMS Scheduler and the SMS Scheduler logo are registered trademarks of SMS Scheduler, used with permission.

Enter the recipient's number, actual text message and select the date and time in the future at which you wish to send the SMS text message.

It is also possible for you to choose the frequency at which you wish to send the SMS text message. You can either send it just once or repeatedly send it at periodic intervals.

Press the **Add** button and the SMS text message will automatically be sent at the defined date and time without any intervention from you.

Unfortunately there is no similar app available for iOS devices, since iOS does not allow third-party apps to be able to automatically send messages without any intervention from the user.

50. HOW TO REMEMBER WHERE YOU PARKED YOUR CAR

 < 60 Seconds

Have you ever walked around in circles inside the parking lot at the shopping mall or airport trying to find where you parked your car? Not being able to remember where you have parked your car is a very common problem. In fact, it is so common that they have even made an entire *Seinfeld* episode about it. However, with the **Car Locator** app on your phone, you will never to worry about forgetting when you parked your car.

Car Locator can be downloaded from the Google Play App Store. The free version allows you to try out the app a few times, after which you will need to buy the app to be able to continue to use it.

Car Locator and the Car Locator logo are registered trademarks of Lindy Labs, used with permission.

Once you have parked your car, you can save its exact GPS location on your phone by launching the **Car Locator** app and pressing the button where a man is holding a flag. As soon as you save the location of your car, it will show up on the screen in the form of a red dot. You can also tap on the camera button on the bottom left corner of the app to take a photo of the location where you have parked your car.

Car Locator and the Car Locator logo are registered trademarks of Lindy Labs, used with permission.

Once you are done with your work and want to locate your car, simply start the app again. You will notice that the screen is split into two views—a radar view and a map view. The red dot that you see on both the screens indicates where your car is parked and the centre of the radar (in the radar view) and green dot in the map view indicates your present location. Just keep looking at the app and keep moving towards the car. You can even tap the **Details** button to get more information about your car's location.

The only limitation of this app is that it will not work as effectively if you are in an area where the GPS signal is not very strong. In case the GPS signals are weak, the **Car Locator** app allows you to manually set the location of the car on the map. Moreover, if you have parked your car in a multi-level parking lot, then this app won't be able to tell you on which level you parked your car. In such a case, taking a photo using the **Camera** feature in the **Car Locator** app can still help you locate your car.

With **Car Locator** on your phone, you no longer need to worry about not being able to find your car in a parking lot. On the other hand, if you are using an iPhone, then **Parkbud (www.parkbud.com)** and **Automatic (www.automatic.com)** are fantastic car-finding apps that I would like to recommend.

51. HOW TO CATCH A CHEATING PARTNER RED-HANDED

 < 120 Seconds

Are you worried that your partner or spouse may be cheating on you? Do you wish there was a way you could spy upon everything on their mobile phone and catch them red-handed? If someone is cheating on you, chances are that you will be able to find some kind of evidence about it on their mobile phone. Your partner's mobile phone would normally contain information about almost everything they do in their lives including who they talk to, where they go, who they message, what websites they visit, photos and videos they take and just about everything else. It is very easy for you to use a spying app to remotely monitor someone else's activities on their mobile phone, including:

1. Call history
2. Intercepting and listen to phone calls
3. Text messages
4. GPS tracking of physical location
5. BBM, WhatsApp and email messages
6. Pictures
7. Videos
8. Recording conversation in their room using the microphone on their phone.
9. SIM card change notification

FlexiSpy (www.flexispy.com), **MobileSpy (www.mobile-spy.com)** and **SpyPhoneGold (www.spyphonegold.com)** are some of the most popular spying apps available on the Internet that allow you to remotely record, monitor and spy upon all activities on someone else's mobile phone. These spying tools work on all popular smartphone platforms like iPhone, iPad, BlackBerry, Android, Windows and others.

To start spying on your partner's mobile phone, simply register an account on any of the above-mentioned spying app websites. It is important to note that since spying apps are hugely popular, all the above-mentioned tools will charge you a registration fee.

Now you need to gain physical access to your partner's mobile phone for a few minutes. You can do this when they are not looking, or pretend to borrow their phone to make a quick phone call.

Using their phone, connect to the spying app website, log in to your account, download and install it on their mobile phone. Once successfully installed, return the phone to your partner.

You can now log in to your online account on the spying app website from anywhere in the world and spy upon everything on your partner's mobile phone!

You can also use these spying apps to keep an eye on what your kids are doing on their mobile phones. Just keep in mind that the usage of such apps may be considered violation of privacy, so check with your local legal authorities before you go ahead with them.

52. HOW TO BLOCK CALLS FROM ANNOYING PEOPLE

 < 120 Seconds

Call Control and the Call Control logo are registered trademarks of Kedlin Inc., used with permission.

Do you receive annoying phone calls from miscreants who simply want to trouble you at odd hours of the day and night? Does your jilted ex-lover refuse to move on and call you incessantly? If you are constantly getting phone calls from annoying people, it can be a drain on not only the battery charge on your phone, but also on your mental peace and well-being. Moreover, asking your mobile phone network provider to block calls from a particular number can be quite a cumbersome process.

Fret not—with the **Call Control** app on your Android phone, you can easily control which calls you want to receive and which calls you want to automatically block. Think of it as your very own digital personal assistant who screens all your calls for you and keeps the annoying ones away!

Start the **Call Control** app, tap the **Black List** option and tap the + button to add a new phone number from which you wish to automatically block all incoming phone calls.

Call Control and the Call Control logo are registered trademarks of Kedlin Inc., used with permission.

Enter the number that you wish to block and press the **Save** button to add it to the **Black List**. Once a number has been added to the **Black List** of the **Call Control** app, any calls from it will automatically be rejected.

Call Control and the Call Control logo are registered trademarks of Kedlin Inc., used with permission.

Call Control and the Call Control logo are registered trademarks of Kedlin Inc., used with permission.

To manage the settings of how the **Call Control** app manages call blocks, you can go into the **Settings** option.

With the **Call Control** app on your phone, you no longer need to worry about dealing with annoying phone calls.

53. HOW TO SLEEP BETTER USING YOUR ANDROID PHONE

 < 240 Seconds

Sleep as Android and the Sleep as Android logo are registered trademarks of Sleep as Android, used with permission.

Do you often wake up feeling groggy and tired even though you have had a full night's sleep? Wouldn't it be great if there was an app on your phone that allows you to track your sleep cycles, get better sleep and wake up feeling more refreshed? **Sleep as Android** is a very interesting app for Android devices that allows you to transform how you sleep.

Sleep as Android and the Sleep as Android logo are registered trademarks of Sleep as Android, used with permission.

The **Sleep as Android** app allows you to track how well and how much you are sleeping every night. While sleeping, people usually have two types of alternating phases—light sleep and deep sleep. Using the accelerometer on your phone, the **Sleep as Android** app is able to monitor your sleep cycles and lets you keep a track of them. Whenever you are going to sleep, simply press the **Sleep Tracking** button in the app to start the tracking. Not only that, you can also go into the **Statistics** page and see how many hours you are sleeping every night and between what times.

This app not only allows you to monitor your sleep cycles to make sure that you are getting enough sleep, but it also has a **Smart Wake Up** option that helps you wake up at the optimal time so that you do not feel groggy and tired. Regular alarm clocks will normally wake you up at the time you set them for, irrespective of whether you are in the middle of light sleep or deep sleep. If you are woken up while you are in deep sleep, chances are you are going to feel groggy, tired and sleepy for the rest of the day. Instead, being woken up while you are in light sleep is more natural and will make you feel relaxed and refreshed from the good night's sleep.

All you need to do for this is specify a time range in which you want to be woken up. Using the accelerometer on your phone, the **Sleep as Android** app will monitor your sleep cycle throughout the night and will wake you up at an optimal time, keeping in the mind the

Sleep as Android and the Sleep as Android logo are registered trademarks of Sleep as Android, used with permission.

time range in which you want to be woken up and your deep and light sleep cycles. Simply set the alarm clock to the latest time you wish to be woken up and then go into **Settings** > **Smart Wake Up** > **Smart Period** and specify how much time before your alarm clock time you want the app to start looking for an optimal time to wake you up.

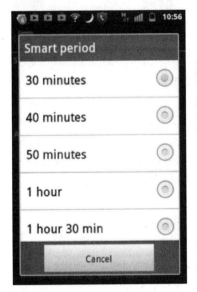

Sleep as Android and the Sleep as Android logo are registered trademarks of Sleep as Android, used with permission.

If you are the type of person who finds it difficult to wake up on time with conventional alarm clocks, this app comes up with tougher-to-ignore alarm clocks known as **CAPTCHA** alarms. For example, you can set an alarm in such a way that to turn the alarm off you will be either required to solve a puzzle or mathematical question or required to vigorously shake your phone. To enable **CAPTCHA** alarm, go into **Settings in the Alarm** tab of the **Sleep as Android** app > **Enable the CAPTCHA option** and then choose the type of **CAPTCHA** alarm you want to use.

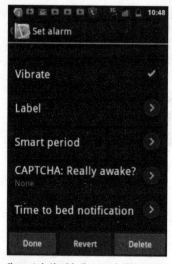 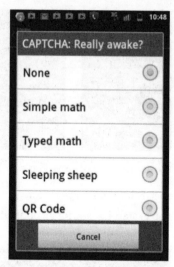

Sleep as Android and the Sleep as Android logo are registered trademarks of Sleep as Android, used with permission.

There is also a feature in this app that allows you to record your sleep-talking and snoring noises. This feature is especially useful if you have a partner who refuses to believe that they were snoring or sleep-talking!

Sleep as Android and the Sleep as Android logo are registered trademarks of Sleep as Android, used with permission.

If you have trouble getting to sleep at night, the **Sleep as Android** app also allows you to choose to play lullaby background sounds like Whales Diving, Thunderstorm, Mountain Stream, Fireplace, Old Clock and many others which will relax you and allow you to fall asleep faster.

Sleep as Android and the Sleep as Android logo are registered trademarks of Sleep as Android, used with permission.

54. HOW TO QUICKLY SWITCH BETWEEN APPS

 < 120 Seconds

Usually when you are using an app in Android, to switch to another app, you need to first go to the home screen. This can be quite a time-consuming and inefficient process. There is a much faster and cooler way. **SwipePad** is a free app that can be downloaded from the Google Play App Store. Once installed on your Android device, it allows you to switch between apps on your phone very quickly and easily with a simple swipe of your finger.

SwipePad and the SwipePad logo are the registered trademarks of SwipePad, used with permission.

Once installed on your phone, **SwipePad** allows you to choose the regions on your screen you want to convert into hotspot regions which, once swiped, will activate a custom-designed quick launch shortcut menu. Simply start **SwipePad** and go to the **Hotspots** tab and then configure all the hotspots regions you want to activate on your phone screen. **SwipePad** supports a total of nine different predefined regions on the screen, each of which can be activated to open a different launch pad containing different shortcuts of your choice.

SwipePad and the SwipePad logo are the registered trademarks of SwipePad, used with permission.

Once you have configured a hotspot region on your phone, tap on that region and, without releasing your finger, move it towards the centre of the screen. You will notice that a launch pad automatically appears on the screen. The first time you create a hotspot region, the launch pad will be completely empty.

SwipePad and the SwipePad logo are the registered trademarks of SwipePad, used with permission.

SwipePad and the SwipePad logo are the registered trademarks of SwipePad, used with permission.

To add or edit a shortcut on the launch pad, hold your finger on the shortcut region for more than two seconds and release when it turns orange. You will now be given the option to add or edit the shortcut to any app of your choice.

Once you have added all the shortcuts of your choice to the launch pad, the next time you swipe your finger in the hotspot region, you will be able to easily switch to any app of your choice. Just release your finger once it is on the shortcut you wish to launch and that app will get launched. With **SwipePad** on your phone, you no longer need to go to the home screen to switch to some other app. Irrespective of what you are doing on your mobile device, just swipe your finger in the hotspot region instead!

With **SwipePad** on your mobile device, switching between apps will become a breeze.

If you are using an iOS device, to smartly switch between apps, you don't need any third-party app. Instead, simply double press the **Home** button to reveal all the recently used apps in the bottom bar of the screen.

55. HOW TO ACCESS WEBSITES NORMALLY AVAILABLE ONLY IN A PARTICULAR REGION

 < 180 Seconds

There are various websites on the Internet that provide free and legal access to your favourite TV shows, music, movies, news and other content. Unfortunately, most of these websites have restrictions that only allow people from a particular region or country to be able to access theor content. This can be quite frustrating. If anyone from outside the 'allowed' region or country tries to access such a website, they are greeted with an error message. In such a case, if you still want to access the website, you need to somehow disguise your location and pretend to be in the 'allowed' region.

This is where something known as a VPN or a Virtual Private Network comes in handy. Using a VPN, is it possible for you to pretend to be located in some other part of the world (like the USA, for example). And once you are able to do that, you will also be able to access all the content on the region-restricted website without paying any money.

A VPN is typically used by companies and organizations to allow their employees to remotely connect to their central office network from anywhere in the world. For example, let us assume that you work for a company that is headquartered in Singapore. If you are travelling to Japan, the United States or Brazil for work and want to access your files, folders, database, printers and other network resources back in your Singapore headquarters, you can use a VPN.

However, there are several public VPNs available on the Internet that can be used to disguise your location (in technical parlance, they allow you to change the IP address of your computer) and pretend to be in some other part of the world. In other words, if you directly connect to a website then you will not be allowed to access the content on it, since the website will know from your IP address that you are outside the 'allowed' region. However, if you first connect to a VPN service based in an 'allowed' region, the website will get fooled and will give you access to all its content for free. As simple as that!

For this example, let us assume that you want to access content on a website that is normally only available to users in the USA. One of my favourite public free VPN services is **HotSpot Shield (http://hotspotshield.com)**. It is a free VPN service, supported by some basic light ads, that establishes a secure encrypted VPN connection between your computer and their Internet gateway, hence giving you full unrestricted access to everything on the Internet. Most of their servers are located in the USA, so by connecting to the **Hotspot Shield** VPN service, you can change your identity and seem to be located in the USA.

Hotspot Shield can be downloaded from **http://hotspotshield.com** and installation takes only a few minutes. Once **Hotspot Shield** has been installed on your computer, you need to start it to tunnel all Internet traffic from all apps on your computer through their server. It is very user-friendly and you don't need to be a techie to be able to use it. There is no configuration of settings that is required.

Hotspot Shield and the Hotspot Shield logo are registered trademarks of AnchorFree Inc., used with permission.

Once **Hotspot Shield** is running in the background on your computer, whenever you launch any app on your computer, it will

Hotspot Shield and the Hotspot Shield logo are registered trademarks of AnchorFree Inc., used with permission.

automatically route your Internet access through the VPN server of **Hotspot Shield** in the USA.

If you want to make sure that your identity and location has been changed to that of a USA-based system, simply start your browser and connect to the website **http://www.whatismyipaddress.com**. When I open this website on my computer, it reveals that my IP address is 64.145.82.169 and my location is California, USA even though I am actually in India!

Hotspot Shield and the Hotspot Shield logo are registered trademarks of AnchorFree Inc., used with permission.

Now that you have successfully changed your location, you can easily bypass the region restriction placed by various websites and access all your favourite TV shows, movies, music, games, news and other content for free. It is also possible to connect your laptop to your LCD or plasma TV to watch the HD-quality episodes on the big screen with surround sound audio.

Once you are done accessing the content, you can disconnect from the **HotSpot Shield** VPN network by clicking on its icon in the taskbar notification area.

LOOK AND FEEL

56. HOW TO SEARCH VISUALLY

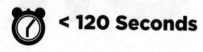 **< 120 Seconds**

Google Images and the Google Images logo are registered trademarks of Google Inc., used with permission.

Have you ever come across a photo and wished there was a way to get more information about it? Maybe you are reading a magazine and see a beautiful hotel or some exotic beach in an ad, and you really want to know where it is. Wouldn't it be great if there was a way to upload a photo of something that you like and get information about it? **Google Images (http://images.google.com)** allows you to search for photos similar to a photo that you already have.

Once you have opened the **Google Images** website, simply click on the camera image in the input box to reveal the various search options. You can either upload a photo of your choice or paste the URL web address of a photo and submit it to Google, so that it can start the visual search.

Google Images and the Google Images logo are registered trademarks of Google Inc., used with permission.

In this example, I have taken a picture of a beautiful landscape photo that I found in a magazine, and uploaded it. I want to find out where this place is and plan my next holiday there. I have to click on the **Upload an image** feature and then click on the **Search** button.

Google Images and the Google Images logo are registered trademarks of Google Inc., used with permission.

Within a few seconds, **Google Images** shows me the search result that the picture that I uploaded is of Machu Picchu in Peru. It shows me some websites where I can read about Machu Picchu, and provides a bunch of other pictures of Machu Picchu. Since Machu Picchu is one of the Wonders of the World, in the search results, Google also shows me pictures of some of the other Wonders of the World. You could also do this for images of products that you see online.

57. HOW TO RESIZE PICTURES EASILY

 **< 180 Seconds**

Most popular websites on the Internet (Facebook, Twitter, LinkedIn and others) require you to submit photos in a particular size, resolution and style. You might then have to fiddle around with some primitive apps to manually resize your photos. Eventually, you will get a photo that fits the website's requirements, but maybe you don't like it. This is where the website **PicResize (www.picresize.com)** can be used. It allows you to edit your photos from any format into any other size, resolution or style of your choice in a matter of a few minutes.

Open your browser and connect to **PicResize**. This website allows you to resize any photo located on your hard drive or the Internet. You

PicResize and the PicResize logo are registered trademarks of Internich LLC, used with permission.

can either drag and drop the photo into this website tool or enter the photo's URL. To upload the selected photo to **PicResize**, click on the **Continue** button.

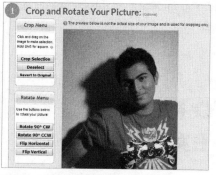

Once you have uploaded the photo to the **PicResize**, as a first step, it will give you the option to crop your photo and rotate it in any direction.

Next, you need to select the final size to which

PicResize and the PicResize logo are registered trademarks of Internich LLC, used with permission.

you want to resize your photo. You can either select from any of the sizes available in the drop-down list, or you can choose to enter a custom size.

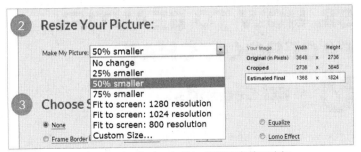

PicResize and the PicResize logo are registered trademarks of Internich LLC, used with permission.

As an optional feature, **PicResize** also allows you to add several special effects to your resized photo.

PicResize and the PicResize logo are registered trademarks of Internich LLC, used with permission.

Finally, you need to select the format in which you want the final resized photo. You can also choose to specify a

PicResize and the PicResize logo are registered trademarks of Internich LLC, used with permission.

maximum size for the final photo, if required. Once you are done, click on the **I'm Done, Resize My Picture!** button.

Within a few seconds, your photo will be resized according to the options that you selected and will be available for your download.

58. HOW TO BEAUTIFY FACEBOOK CHAT

 **< 60 Seconds**

If you spend a lot of time chatting with your friends on Facebook Chat, chances are that you would get bored of its plain-looking interface. It is possible to completely customize the look and feel of the Facebook Chat interface to suit your preferences using the **Pretty Facebook Chat** browser app.

Pretty Facebook Chat and the Pretty Facebook Chat logo are registered trademarks of Luca Rainone, used with permission.

You can install **Pretty Facebook Chat** from the Google Chrome Web Store. Unfortunately, this app is currently not available for any browser except Google Chrome. Once installed, the next time you go to your Facebook account, you will see a new icon in the URL address bar of your browser and also next to the Facebook Chat window in the bottom right corner of your browser. You can use these icons to change the various settings related to **Pretty Facebook Chat**, and also switch it on and off.

One of the most useful features of **Pretty Facebook Chat** is that it adds hundreds of smileys, memes and special letters to your Facebook Chat that are normally not available. Installing this app will surely make your Facebook Chat experience a lot more fun. You can also use **Pretty Facebook Chat** to completely customize

Pretty Facebook Chat and the Pretty Facebook Chat logo are registered trademarks of Luca Rainone, used with permission.

the look and feel of the Facebook Chat messages that you send to your friends (text size, colour, font family etc.) and the Facebook Chat window in which you are chatting (window size, shadow effect, location on screen and theme). For example, using this browser app, you can send chat messages in different colours and styles with the background in a special theme, like the *Hello Kitty* theme.

59. HOW TO CUSTOMIZE EVERYTHING IN YOUTUBE

 < 120 Seconds

YouTube has become one of the most popular video-viewing and sharing platforms in the world. Every month, there are hundreds of millions of unique users who view videos on YouTube. A limitation associated with YouTube is that it normally does not allow users to customize its look and feel, functionality and features. But the true power of a platform like YouTube can only be experienced when you are able to completely customize it to suit your personal needs and preferences. There is a very useful browser app called **YouTube Options**, which is available as a free download for both Google Chrome and Mozilla Firefox.

YouTube Options and the YouTube Options logo are registered trademarks of YouTube LLC, used with permission.

Once you have installed the **YouTube Options** app in your browser, the **YTO** icon will appear in the URL address bar each time you go to YouTube. When you click on the **YTO** icon, a console interface will show up on the screen that will allow you to control just about everything related to your YouTube video-watching experience, including:

1. Size and resolution of videos
YouTube Options allows you to completely customize the size and resolution of any video that you are watching.

2. Advertisements
If you don't like to watch the annoying ads before the start of YouTube videos, then you can choose to disable them using **YouTube Options**.

3. Look and feel of the YouTube screen

You can also control everything that gets displayed on the YouTube screen along with your video. You can get rid of anything that you don't like. For example, you can get rid of YouTube comments and suggested videos vertical column.

4. Automatic loop

If you want to keep watching a video over and over again, then you should turn the loop option to On.

5.Auto-play and Auto-buffer

Using these options, you can choose to enable or disable auto-play and auto-buffer of the videos that you watch on YouTube.

Although most of the features available in **YouTube Options** are designed to work only on YouTube, many of them are even supported on other video platforms like Vimeo, DailyMotion, MetaCafe and Hulu.

60. HOW TO IMPROVE YOUR PHOTO-VIEWING EXPERIENCE ON FACEBOOK

 < 60 Seconds

Most of us have spent endless hours looking at other people's photos on Facebook. Normally, when you are looking at photos on Facebook, you have to click on each photo individually to open and view it. However, there is a faster and better way to view photos on Facebook using the **Photo Zoom for Facebook** browser extension. It is available on both Google Chrome and Mozilla Firefox browsers, and you can install it from the Chrome Web Store (https://chrome.google.com) or the Mozilla Firefox add-ons website (https://addons.mozilla.org).

Once you have installed **Photo Zoom for Facebook**, you can see a larger version of any photo on Facebook simply by hovering your mouse over it for a few seconds. If you are viewing your friend's photo album, the usually miniature versions of all the photos in that album are displayed on a single page. However, it is possible for you now to quickly view a large maximized version of any of the photos in the album by hovering the mouse cursor over the photo for a few seconds.

Similarly, even within your Facebook feed, it is possible to see a larger version of your friends' profile pictures by simply hovering your mouse cursor over their picture for a few seconds. With the help of **Photo Zoom for Facebook**, your photo-viewing experience on Facebook will improve significantly.

61. HOW TO ADD SPECIAL EFFECTS TO TEXT ON FACEBOOK AND TWITTER

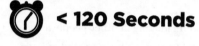 **< 120 Seconds**

Usually, social networking websites do not give you too many options to customize how the text that you enter (status updates, tweets, comments, wall posts etc.) will end up looking. If you want to add special effects to text entered by you on social networking websites to surprise your friends, this tip is just for you.

You don't need to restrict the language that you enter text in to English—it is even possible to write on your favourite social networking sites in various regional languages. Start

Google Transliteration and the Google Transliteration logo are registered trademarks of Google Inc., used with permission.

your browser and connect to **Google Transliteration (http://www.google.com/transliterate)** and select the Hindi language option from the drop-down menu. This website allows you to type in English, but will then automatically convert the text into the regional language you have chosen. In the space provided, type the text. The trick to remember here is that you need to think of the text in Hindi, but write it in English. As you are typing, whenever you press the spacebar key, **Google Transliteration** will automatically convert your text into Hindi.

Copy the text and paste it into your favourite social networking site, e.g. Facebook. You will notice that your Facebook status has been updated in Hindi. You can also click on the drop-down

Google Transliteration and the Google Transliteration logo are registered trademarks of Google Inc., used with permission.

button in **Google Transliteration** and select any other language of your choice.

It is also possible for you to write text in reverse in various places on popular social networking websites. For this effect, start your browser and connect to the website **Reverse Text Generator (http://textmechanic.com/Reverse-Text-Generator.html)**. In the space provided, simply type any text of your choice, and then, choose from any of the special effects buttons at the top.

62. HOW TO GATHER INFORMATION AS YOU TRAVEL USING YOUR MOBILE PHONE

 < 270 Seconds

Google has completely changed the way we look for and access information. Google allows users to search for information in a variety of different ways. My favourite search method on Google is to use **Google Goggles**.

Google Goggles and the Google Goggles logo are registered trademarks of Google Inc., used with permission.

Google Goggles is a free mobile app that can be downloaded from **Google Mobile (http://www. google.com/mobile/ goggles/)** and runs on both the Android and the iOS platforms. Once installed, it allows you to take photos of everyday objects and landmarks around you and instantly search for more information about them. It only requires you to have a data Internet access on your mobile phone.

Google Goggles and the Google Goggles logo are registered trademarks of Google Inc., used with permission.

Google Goggles and the Google Goggles logo are registered trademarks of Google Inc., used with permission.

There are many everyday situations in which **Google Goggles** ends up being a very useful app. Imagine that you are exploring a foreign country and, while walking around, you see an interesting building and want to know the history of it. All you need to do is take a picture of it using **Google Goggles** and automatically Google will give you more information about it.

To use this feature, start the **Google Goggles** app on your mobile phone. In this example, I am going to use an Android phone.

I have taken a photo of the monument about which I seek more information. **Google Goggles** will now scan the entire photo and try to identify the monument. It will also make use of my physical location (through the GPS feature on my phone) while trying to identify the monument in the photo.

Within a few seconds, **Google Goggles** recognizes the monument in the photo as the famous Chichen Itza pyramid in Mexico and displays links at the bottom to pages where I can get more information about it.

Google Goggles and the Google Goggles logo are registered trademarks of Google Inc., used with permission.

Clicking on any of those links will allow me to get more information about the Chichen Itza pyramid. You can get information about the history, background, location, directions and other details about a place with a single photo! This will work not only with very famous monuments, but also with lesser-known landmarks and locations.

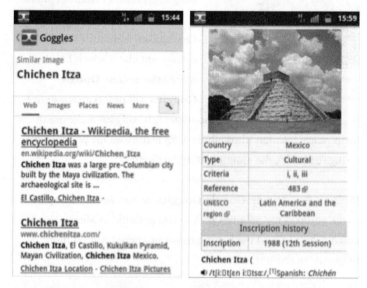

Google Goggles and the Google Goggles logo are registered trademarks of Google Inc., used with permission.

After a few hours of walking around, if you get hungry and decide to get lunch, only to realize that the menus are in a foreign language, once again, all you need to do is take a picture of the menu and **Google Goggles** instantly converts it into the language of your choice! No need to feel foreign in a foreign country again.

If you walk into a bookstore and see an interesting book and want to see what kind of reviews the book has received online and whether there are cheaper prices available online from other bookstores, all you need to do is take a picture of the book cover using **Google Goggles** and it will instantly display reviews, prices from various websites and a lot of other

Google Goggles and the Google Goggles logo are registered trademarks of Google Inc., used with permission.

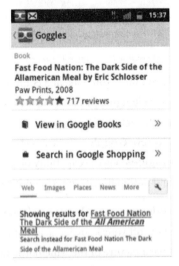

Google Goggles and the Google Goggles logo are registered trademarks of Google Inc., used with permission.

information about the book.

Once you are back at the hotel, if you notice a pillow cover that you really like and want to find out if something similar is available online, once again **Google Goggles** will come to your rescue. Just take a photo of the pillow cover and feed it into **Google Goggles**. If it is available online, **Google Goggles** will identify it and give you links to the website from where you can order it for your home!

Google Goggles and the Google Goggles logo are registered trademarks of Google Inc., used with permission.

If you meet someone at a conference or a business meeting, instead of exchanging physical business cards and then manually entering all the data into your computer or mobile phone, you can simply use **Google Goggles**. Take a picture of the business card, and **Google Goggles** has the capability of recognizing the information from it and automatically entering it into the address book of your phone.

Ordering a fancy bottle of wine at a classy restaurant and want to show off your knowledge about the history of the wine? Simple— take a picture of the wine bottle using **Google Goggles**! While writing this book, I tried **Google Goggles** on numerous bottles of

wine, but did not get successful results each time. I imagine that Google is still perfecting this feature.

Overall, this is quite an interesting and useful app that allows you to make better sense of the world around with a simple picture!

Google Goggles and the Google Goggles logo are registered trademarks of Google Inc., used with permission.

63. HOW TO CUSTOMIZE THE BACKGROUND AND COLOURS ON FACEBOOK

 < 60 Seconds

If you are not happy with the plain white background that is normally visible on all Facebook accounts, it is possible for you to change it to something that you prefer. Install the **Facebook Background Changer** browser app in your Google Chrome browser from the Google Chrome Web Store (https://chrome. google.com/webstore). It will add a new icon to the address bar of your browser, which will automatically appear only when you visit Facebook. If you are using Mozilla Firefox, you can use the **Stylish** browser app to change the background in Facebook.

To use the Chrome app, click on the **Facebook Background Changer** icon and you will be able to change the background by choosing from its database of images. You can also upload a photo from your own computer. Besides, you can also change the colour of the header bar that appears at the top of all Facebook pages.

64. HOW TO DOWNLOAD ENTIRE PHOTO ALBUMS FROM FACEBOOK

 < 180 Seconds

Facebook has become the primary platform for most of us to upload, view and share photo albums with our friends and family members. However, although it is possible to download individual photos from a friend's Facebook profile to your computer, you cannot download an entire photo album at once—you need to open and download every single photo in that album individually. Imagine how long it will take to download a photo album with a hundred different photos!

SocialFolders and the SocialFolders logo are registered trademarks of SocialFolders Inc., used with permission.

SocialFolders is a free app available at **http://socialfolders.me**. It allows you to download, manage and even upload photos across all photo-sharing social networking platforms like Facebook, Twitter, Instagram, Flickr, Picasa and others.

SocialFolders and the SocialFolders logo are registered trademarks of SocialFolders Inc., used with permission.

Once installed, the **SocialFolders** icon will appear at the bottom right corner of your desktop in the Windows taskbar. Right-click on it, and select the **Manage My Channels** option. This will open the web interface of the **SocialFolders** app in your browser, where you will be able to manage all the different websites on which you wish to download, manage and upload photos.

Click on the **Add a new service** button to connect **SocialFolders** to any social networking platform of your choice. In this example, since we want to download an entire photo album from Facebook, I have selected Facebook.

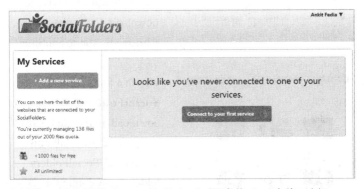

SocialFolders and the SocialFolders logo are registered trademarks of SocialFolders Inc., used with permission.

Facebook will now ask you if you wish to allow **SocialFolders** to access content from your Facebook account or not. Click on the **Go to App** button and select whatever permissions you would like to provide to the **SocialFolders** app.

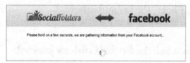

SocialFolders and the SocialFolders logo are registered trademarks of SocialFolders Inc., used with permission.

Once **SocialFolders** has connected to your Facebook account, it will allow you to select all the photo albums you wish to download from it. Select as many photo albums as you want and click on the **I'm Done** button to continue.

SocialFolders and the SocialFolders logo are registered trademarks of SocialFolders Inc., used with permission.

Not only does **SocialFolders** allow you to download entire photo albums from your own Facebook account, but in the next step, it will also allow you to select any photo albums of your friends that you wish to download as well. Once I have selected all the photo albums I wish to download, I will click on the **Choose** button to continue.

SocialFolders and the SocialFolders logo are registered trademarks of SocialFolders Inc., used with permission.

Within a few minutes, **SocialFolders** will download all the photos from the selected photo albums to a special 'SocialFolders' folder on my computer. This folder can be accessed in the 'My Documents' folder of my computer. On my computer, the path of the folder is **C:\Users\ankitfadia\ Documents\SocialFolders**.

SocialFolders and the SocialFolders logo are registered trademarks of SocialFolders Inc., used with permission.

Not only does **SocialFolders** make it easy for you to download pictures from photo-sharing platforms, it also makes it very easy for you to share photos from one platform to another. If, after downloading the photo album, I want to share it with some other friends on Picasa, I need to simply connect **SocialFolders** to Picasa, just the way I connected it earlier to Facebook. Then, I will go to the special SocialFolders folder on my computer, copy the photo album from the Facebook folder and paste it into the Picasa folder. Within a few minutes, **SocialFolders** will automatically upload the photo album from my computer to my Picasa account.

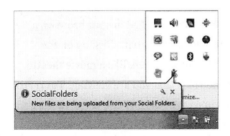

SocialFolders and the SocialFolders logo are registered trademarks of SocialFolders Inc., used with permission.

The best thing about **SocialFolders** is that it is very intuitive and user-friendly. The moment you start uploading photos from your computer to a website, you will be shown a notification in the Windows taskbar. It will also notify you once the upload has been successfully completed.

65. HOW TO GET THE MOVIE-THEATRE EFFECT WHILE WATCHING YOUTUBE VIDEOS

 < 60 Seconds

It is possible to add a movie-theatre effect on YouTube such that the entire screen except the video will get dimmed whenever you are watching a video. There is a browser extension called **Turn Off the Lights** that is available for both the Google Chrome and Mozilla Firefox browsers.

Once **Turn off the Lights** has been installed in your browser, a lamp icon will appear in your URL address bar. Clicking on the lamp icon will help you dim the entire screen, like a movie theatre, and put complete focus on the video that you are viewing. **Turn Off the Lights** will drastically improve your YouTube video-viewing experience by giving it a movie-theatre effect.

66. HOW TO EXPLORE THE NIGHT SKY USING YOUR PHONE

 < 60 Seconds

Have you ever looked up to the sky and wondered which stars, constellations and planets are visible just above you? We tend to notice stars while on vacation away from the city. Most of us don't know what we are looking at when we look at the sky, but some of us would like to be more celestially aware.

Sky Map and the Sky Map logo are registered trademarks of Google Inc., used with permission.

Sky Map is an interesting Android app developed by Google which allows you to identify things that you see in the sky. It is available as a free download from **http://www.google.com/mobile/skymap**. Based on the GPS coordinates, the in-built compass and the clock in your mobile phone, **Sky Map** is able to identify celestial bodies when you point your phone at the sky. **Sky Map** gets automatically updated as you move. It will also allow you to search for specific bodies that you want to locate in the sky. Just download and install **Sky Map** on your Android phone and start playing with it by pointing it in different directions in the sky. In the example above, I have been able to identify various planets (Mercury, Venus, Jupiter, Pluto), stars and constellations that are currently above me in the sky.

67. HOW TO DOWNLOAD VIDEOS FROM YOUTUBE

 < 120 Seconds

There are more than two billion videos viewed on YouTube every day. Anyone with an Internet-enabled device can easily upload and share videos with the world in a matter of minutes. But one restriction that YouTube imposes on its users is that you are not allowed to download any videos. Wouldn't it be amazing if you could do that?

There are a number of video-downloading websites like **Savevid (www.savevid.com)**, **Keepvid (www.keepvid.com)** and **Zamzar (www.zamzar.com)** that allow you to download videos from popular video-streaming websites. Just copy-paste the URL of the streaming video that you wish to download into any of these video-downloading websites, choose the format you want the downloaded video to be in and start downloading.

For example, start your browser and connect to **Savevid.com**. In the space provided enter the URL web address of any video that you wish to download and click on download. The website will retrieve the videos and you will be given the option to download it in any format of your choice (.flv, .mp4 etc.). Select the format and click on the **Download** button to start your download.

Instead of downloading the video, you may also want to extract and download just the audio from a video that you are watching on YouTube. This can be done through a website called **VidtoMP3.com**

(http://www.vidtoMP3.com). Once you connect to this website, simply copy-paste the web address of the video from which you wish to extract and download the audio portion, and click on the **Download** button.

68. HOW TO CUSTOMIZE THE LOOK AND FEEL OF FACEBOOK

 < 120 Seconds

If you are not happy with the look and feel of Facebook, it is possible for you to completely customize it based on your personal preferences. Facebook users are normally not given any options to customize their Facebook accounts. This is where the **Social Fixer** browser app comes into the picture. It works on almost all the popular browsers, and allows users to completely alter the visual aspect of their Facebook account.

Social Fixer and the Social Fixer logo are registered trademarks of Social Fixer, used with permission.

Open the **Social Fixer** website **(http://socialfixer.com)** and select the browser you are using, to download the app to your computer.

Once you have installed **Social Fixer** in your browser, it automatically adds a new icon to the Facebook navigation bar at the top of your browser. You can use this to control the various options of the **Social Fixer** app.

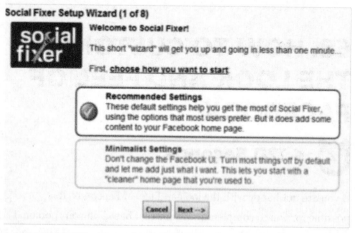

Some of the most useful features of Social Fixer are the following:

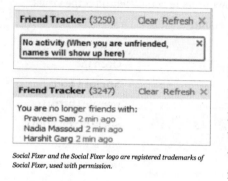

1. Find out who unfriends you on Facebook

Social Fixer adds a **Friend Tracker** box to your Facebook account, which allows you to keep track of all your friends, including finding out if someone has unfriended you on Facebook.

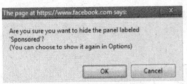

2. Remove all ads from Facebook

Social Fixer will put a cross button on top of the ads column in your Facebook account. You can click on it to remove all ads from your Facebook account.

3. Customize what gets displayed on your Facebook feed

You can customize what gets displayed on your Facebook feed.

4. Customize the look of your friends' profiles

You can customize the look and feel of your friends' profile pages.

SECU
RITY

69. HOW TO DETECT IF YOUR ACCOUNT HAS BEEN HACKED

 < 120 Seconds

Nowadays most people have extremely confidential documents, emails, pictures, links and private stuff in their email account. The very thought of someone else being able to access your email account and go through your private stuff can be quite scary. Have you ever been in a situation where you feel that someone else knows things about you that were not mentioned anywhere other than in your email account? Do you suspect that your email account has been hacked and someone is spying upon you? If you are in any of these inconvenient situations, or are just obsessive about maintaining the privacy and security of your email account, then this is the tip for you.

Last account activity: 10 minutes ago
Details

Gmail and the Gmail logo are registered trademarks of Google Inc., used with permission.

1. Gmail

In Gmail, there is a **Last Account Activity** feature that allows you to get information about when, how and from where your account was accessed in the last few sessions. This information can be very useful to figure out if someone has been illegally accessing your account. To get the last account activity details, log in to your Gmail account, scroll to the bottom and click on the **Details** link below where it says **Last Account Activity**.

This will open up the entire log-in history of your Gmail account up to the ten most recent log-in sessions. Not only does it tell you the exact date and time when your account was accessed, it also reveals the location of the IP address from where it was accessed and from what kind of a device it was accessed. By analysing this log-in history, you can find out about any illegitimate log-in to your account in the last few sessions.

Activity on this account

This feature provides information about the last activity on this mail account and any concurrent activity. Learn more

This account does not seem to be open in any other location. However, there may be sessions that have not been signed out.

Sign out all other sessions

Recent activity:

Access Type [?] (Browser, mobile, POP3, etc.)	Location (IP address) [?]	Date/Time (Displayed in your time zone)
Browser (Chrome) Show details	* India (MH) (121.245.145.229)	5:14 pm (0 minutes ago)
Mobile	178.239.83.150	5:13 pm (1 minute ago)
Mobile	178.239.83.150	4:25 pm (49 minutes ago)
Mobile	178.239.83.150	3:27 pm (1.5 hours ago)
Mobile	178.239.83.150	3:09 pm (2 hours ago)
Browser (Chrome) Show details	India (MH) (121.245.145.229)	1:59 pm (3 hours ago)
Mobile	178.239.83.150	1:54 pm (3 hours ago)
Mobile	178.239.83.150	1:38 pm (3.5 hours ago)
Mobile	178.239.83.150	1:11 pm (4 hours ago)
Authorized Application (attachments me) Show details	United States (23.20.45.235)	12:56 pm (4 hours ago)

Alert preference: Show an alert for unusual activity. change

Gmail and the Gmail logo are registered trademarks of Google Inc., used with permission.

For example, the image above shows that my account was last accessed five minutes ago, using a browser from the IP address 108.35.118.245 in the location New Jersey, USA. It was also accessed six minutes ago from an unknown mobile phone with the IP address 178.239.83.150. Maybe it was my BlackBerry phone, but I can't be sure by simply looking at this page, since, if you notice, there is no location that is showing up, nor does it show what kind of mobile phone it was. In such cases, if you want to get more detailed information about the IP address, simply connect to the IP Lookup feature on the website **What Is My IP Address (http://whatismyipaddress.com/ip-lookup).**

Copy-paste the IP address you want to look up in the space provided and click on the **Lookup** button. Within a few seconds, you are likely to be shown something like the following image.

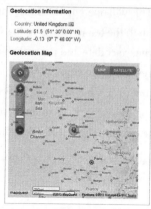

What Is My IP Address and the What Is My IP Address logo are registered trademarks of CGP Holding Inc., used with permission.

This confirms that the unknown IP address is indeed my BlackBerry phone and it is accessing my Gmail account from the UK server of Research in Motion (the company that owns BlackBerry).

In case you come across any suspicious log-ins to your Gmail account, then the best part about the **Last account activity** feature is that you can click on the **Sign out all other sessions** button to end all currently logged-in sessions worldwide except yours. This feature not only logs out any cybercriminal who may have somehow managed to log in to your account, but also allows you to log out from any legitimately logged-in session that you may have forgotten to log out from another computer. For example, in case you had accessed your Gmail account from a hotel business centre computer or a friend's computer but forgot to log out, this feature can be very useful.

This account does not seem to be open in any other location. However, there may be sessions that have not been signed out.

Sign out all other sessions

Gmail and the Gmail logo are registered trademarks of Google Inc., used with permission.

It is highly recommended that you keep track of information in the **Last account activity** page on a regular basis to detect any suspicious activity at your account.

2. Facebook

Facebook allows you to view a history of all logged-in sessions to your account by clicking on **Settings > Account Settings > Security > Active Sessions**. If you notice any active sessions that you did not start, you click on the **End Activity** link to remotely log out from it.

It is also recommended that you enable **Login Notifications** on your Facebook account, so that you receive an email and an SMS text message each time someone logs in to your account from a device that you have not used before. To enable **Login Notifications** on your account, simply go to **Settings > Account Settings > Security > Login Notifications** and enable them.

70. HOW TO MAKE YOUR ACCOUNTS HACK-PROOF

 < 300 Seconds

Have you ever clicked on links received in an email? Have you ever used the same password for all your accounts? Have you ever used a computer other than your own personal computer to log in to your Gmail account? Have you ever downloaded software or music or movies from a dodgy website? If you have done any of this, chances are that, unbeknownst to you, some malicious attacker would have tried to hack into your Gmail account at some point of time.

Hundred per cent security does not exist, but Gmail allows you to get close. If you want to make it almost impossible for a cybercriminal or malicious attacker to hack into your Gmail account, then you need to enable **2-step verification** on it. This unique feature adds an additional layer of security to your Gmail account. As the name suggests, once you enable 2-Step Verification in your Gmail account, there will be two different security layers protecting your Gmail account. In the first step, you will need to enter your username and password as you normally would, and then in the second step you need to enter a special **Verification code** that is sent to your mobile phone via a text message or voice call. Only if the correct information is entered by a user in both the layers of verification is access to the Gmail account provided. This means that the only way a cybercriminal can hack into your Gmail account is if he is able to get your password and also steal your mobile phone from you.

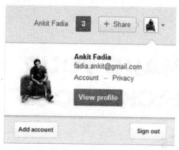

To enable **2-step verification** in your Gmail account, log in to your Gmail account and then click on your name in the top right corner of the screen, and then on the **Account** link, to reveal the **Accounts settings** page for your account.

Gmail and the Gmail logo are registered trademarks of Google Inc., used with permission.

Click on the **Security** option in the left column of your **Account settings** page. This will open up the **Security settings** page for your account, which allows you to manage various security options related to your Gmail account. If you notice, by default the **2-step verification** feature on your Gmail account will be switched off. Simply click on the Edit button to enable it.

Gmail and the Gmail logo are registered trademarks of Google Inc., used with permission.

Gmail and the Gmail logo are registered trademarks of Google Inc., used with permission.

You now need to enter the mobile phone number to which you want Google to send the verification code. Based on your personal preference, you can choose to receive the verification code either via text message or voice call. Now click on the **Send code** button so that Google can send a code to your mobile phone to verify that you have entered a correct mobile phone number.

Once you receive the verification code on your mobile phone either via text message or voice call, you need to enter it in the space provided so that you can verify your mobile phone device.

Gmail and the Gmail logo are registered trademarks of Google Inc., used with permission.

You can choose to be asked to enter the verification code every time you log in to your Gmail account from any computer. You can also choose to get Gmail to trust your current computer, so that you are asked to enter the verification code only whenever someone attempts to log in to your Gmail account from a computer other than your trusted computer.

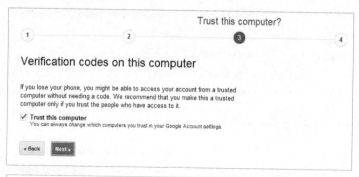

Gmail and the Gmail logo are registered trademarks of Google Inc., used with permission.

Now click on the **Confirm** button to enable the **2-step verification** feature on your Gmail account.

The next time, whenever you attempt to log in to your Gmail account from a trusted computer,

Gmail and the Gmail logo are registered trademarks of Google Inc., used with permission.

you will only be asked for your username and password. However, if you or someone else tries to log into your Gmail account from some other computer, then not only would they be asked for your username and password, but they would also be asked to enter the verification code from your mobile phone.

What happens if you have enabled the **2-step verification** feature on your Gmail account and your mobile phone gets stolen or lost? How do you access your Gmail account? The first thing to do is to log in to your Gmail account from a trusted computer, in which case you will not be asked to enter the verification code from your mobile phone. However, if you are travelling out of the country and cannot get to a trusted computer, how can you still access your Gmail account?

This is where the **Backup phone** feature comes into play. It is possible for you to add a friend or family member's number as the backup phone on your Gmail account. In case of an emergency, you can ask Gmail to send the verification code to the backup phone instead of to your regular phone. This feature ensures that you will still be able to access your Gmail account.

Gmail and the Gmail logo are registered trademarks of Google Inc., used with permission.

Let us imagine an even bigger emergency. You have lost both your regular phone and your backup phone. Or you have lost your phone and, for some reason, you are not able to get in touch with the person who has the backup phone. How can you still access your Gmail account? This is where something known as **Printable backup codes** is helpful. Using this feature, you can print a bunch of backup verification codes and store them in a safe place (like your wallet). These backup codes will be the only way for you to access your Gmail account if both your regular phone and backup phone are misplaced.

Gmail and the Gmail logo are registered trademarks of Google Inc., used with permission.

If you are using an Android, iPhone or BlackBerry mobile phone, then you don't even need to rely on an SMS or voice call to receive your Gmail verification code. Instead, you could install the **2-step verification** mobile app on your phone and it will do the rest.

Mobile application
Switch to an app to get codes even when you don't have cell coverage.

Android - iPhone - BlackBerry ⑦

Gmail and the Gmail logo are registered trademarks of Google Inc., used with permission.

One problem that you may encounter after enabling **2-step verification** is that you may not be able to access your Gmail account from web or mobile apps other than a browser (Google Talk, Picasa, Push Email on your smartphone or tablet, email clients like Outlook). The reason why these other apps no longer work is that they were not designed to have any additional space available for you to enter the verification code. In other words, they are not compatible with the **2-step verification** feature. This is where **Application-specific passwords** come into the picture.

Application-specific passwords

Some applications that access Google Accounts from a phone, desktop, or other devices (like mobile Gmail, desktop Picasa, or AdWords Editor) cannot ask for verification codes.

Manage application-specific passwords

To use these applications, you'll need to enter an application-specific password in the password field instead of your account password. Learn more

Gmail and the Gmail logo are registered trademarks of Google Inc., used with permission.

Gmail and the Gmail logo are registered trademarks of Google Inc., used with permission.

Application-specific passwords are special sixteen-character-long passwords that are generated for specific apps only and cannot be used elsewhere to log in to your Gmail account. **Application-specific passwords** do not need to be memorized by you and only need to be entered once into the app that does not support **2-step verification**. You should remember to enable the **Save password** option in your app, so that you don't need to generate the **Application-specific password** repeatedly.

71. HOW TO AVOID PHISHING ATTACKS

⏰ < 60 Seconds

Phishing is a technique used by cybercriminals who try to steal your confidential information by pretending to be someone you trust. For example, you may receive an email that seems to have been sent by your bank asking for your account details, but in reality would have been sent by a phishing expert. Even though the email seems very real, it is actually sent by a cybercriminal and is an attempt to steal your account password. Phishing attacks have become even more dangerous and sophisticated today, since they accurately replicate the legitimate trusted source. For example, they will have the real logo, will use the same font and will seem to come from a real email address. Typically phishing attacks can be in the following forms:

1. Account upgrade, system maintenance, software crash or some other mundane reason

2. SMS text message that seems as if your bank or relative or friend is trying to get in touch with you

3. Instant message asking you for confidential details about some online account

4. Private message on Facebook containing a link that may take you to a page that looks like a log-in screen for Facebook, but actually is a fake log-in screen that steals your password

There are some simple things that you can keep in mind in order to avoid becoming the victim of a phishing attack:

1. Your bank or credit card company will under no circumstances ask for your password. Really. It will never happen.

2. If the email you have received contains a link, do not blindly click on the link, since it could potentially lead you to a fake log-in screen or a malicious website, or execute some other type of a phishing attack. Before clicking on a link, you can find out where it is going to take you by holding your mouse over it for a few seconds and looking at the status bar of your browser.

3. You may receive an email that contains a link that looks very authentic. Even if you hover your mouse over it, it may seem like the link to a legitimate, trustworthy website. Take a look at the following web address—https://www.icicibank.com@www.xyz123$.com. At first glance this may look like a page on the website of ICICI Bank, but in reality it will take you to a completely different address which begins separately after the @ sign. Such simple URL obfuscation tricks are commonly used by cybercriminals to fool unsuspecting victims. Please do not click on any link in these emails, no matter how genuine and trustworthy it might seem.

4. Even if a link seems safe, if it was sent to you from a dubious source, you should avoid using it to log in to any of your accounts. Whenever you want to log in to any online account (email, bank, social networking site or others), always open the browser in a new window, type the website address and then type the username and password to log in.

5. Always check for 'https' in the URL address bar of your browser, before you enter any confidential details on a website. Typically, only trustworthy websites will use 'https' and phishing websites normally use 'http'.

6. Make sure that you are on a genuine website by carefully reading the URL address bar. Watch out for websites with spellings that are similar to the actual website. For example, make sure you are not on 'online.citibenk.com' instead of 'online.citibank.com'. Cybercriminals are known to register website domain names with a spelling similar to a trusted website.

7. A simple way to differentiate between a real email and a phishing email is to carefully look for your full name mentioned somewhere in the email. Usually, a cybercriminal will not know your full name and will instead use a generic salutation (like 'Sir' or your email address) to address you. If you don't find your full name or some other unique identifier (credit card number, bank account number and others) mentioned anywhere in the email, then you should be suspicious.

8. Another telltale sign to look out for is the fact that a phishing attack email will usually have a number of spelling or grammatical errors.

Google Chrome and the Google Chrome logo are registered trademarks of Google Inc., used with permission.

9. Most popular browsers (like Google Chrome, Mozilla Firefox and Internet Explorer) maintain a list of known phishing websites in their database and warn you whenever you are about to visit any phishing website that appears in their database.

10. Many popular email providers, like Gmail, also have built-in anti-phishing features that will automatically scan all incoming email for things normally found in known phishing scams. Whenever a phishing attack is detected, Gmail will automatically move the email to the spam folder or may display the following message when you try to open the email:

Google Chrome and the Google Chrome logo are registered trademarks of Google Inc., used with permission.

11. If you receive a link and are not sure whether it is safe to click on it or not, you can check whether it has been reported as a suspected phishing website by submitting it to a site called **PhishTank (www.phishtank.com)**. This website maintains a comprehensive list of known phishing websites and provides a quick way to check whether a website appears in that list or not. If your link appears in their database, it is a bad idea to click on it.

PhishTank and the PhishTank logo are registered trademarks of OpenDNS LLC, used with permission.

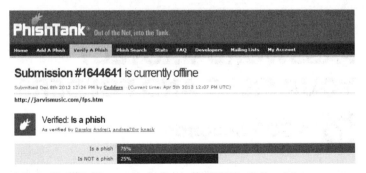

PhishTank and the PhishTank logo are registered trademarks of OpenDNS LLC, used with permission.

12. There are commercial anti-phishing software tools available that provide you protection against phishing attacks. For example, McAfee's **SiteAdvisor Live** is a product that allows you to identify and protect yourself from risky websites. You can buy it online from **http://home.mcafee.com/store/siteadvisor-live**.

13. Most importantly, if you have never opened an account with a particular bank and they email you, then it probably is a phishing attack. No matter how tempting their offer might be, do not click on any of their links.

If you keep these simple tips in mind, you won't have to worry about becoming a victim to a phishing attack.

72. HOW TO ENCRYPT AND PASSWORD-PROTECT YOUR FILES AND FOLDERS

 < 300 Seconds

Sometimes just setting a password on your file is not enough. If a cybercriminal is really motivated and has the right technical knowledge, they can crack this password and gain illegal access to your confidential data. Hence, it is always advisable to encrypt your confidential files and folders with a strong encryption standard. The **TrueCrypt** encryption tool can be used in such situations. It is available as a free download from **http://www.truecrypt.org**.

Before we continue, there are a few computer-related terms that we need to understand properly:

Term	Definition
Virtual Disk	A file that seems like an actual drive to your system
Volume	A finite amount of storage space on a drive (like your hard drive, USB drive etc.)
Mount	Before a computer can use a device or a drive (like a hard drive or CD or pen drive), it has to be mounted so that it becomes accessible to you.

TrueCrypt creates a virtual encrypted disk within a file on your computer and mounts it as a real disk or drive, so that you are allowed to store files on it in encrypted format. You will be allowed to save files on the virtual disk just the way you normally save files on any other disk on your computer. The best thing about **TrueCrypt** is that it does all the encryption on the fly, without causing any time lag in your day-to-day work.

Before you can start storing your files and folders in an encrypted format, you need to create a **TrueCrypt** volume. Think of this as a finite area on your hard drive, inside which all the encrypted data will be stored. To create the volume, start **TrueCrypt** on your computer and click

TrueCrypt and the TrueCrypt logo are registered trademarks of TrueCrypt Developers Association, used with permission.

on the **Create Volume** button. This will start the **TrueCrypt Volume Creation Wizard**.

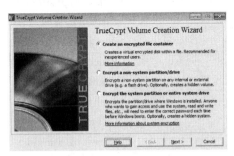

Next, you need to create a virtual disk within any file on your computer. Select the first option which is selected by default, and click on the **Next** button to continue.

TrueCrypt and the TrueCrypt logo are registered trademarks of TrueCrypt Developers Association, used with permission.

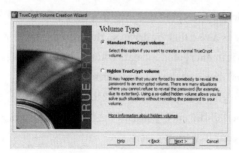

Select the **Standard TrueCrypt Volume** option and click on the **Next** button to continue.

TrueCrypt and the TrueCrypt logo are registered trademarks of TrueCrypt Developers Association, used with permission.

In the next step, you need to select the location on your hard drive where you want to create the **TrueCrypt** container file. Click on the **Select File** button, choose any location and type in the name that you want to give to the **TrueCrypt** container file. Ensure that you type in a new file name and not the name of an existing file, since **TrueCrypt** will completely overwrite whatever file you name. It is important to understand that during this step you are not creating any encrypted files; you are merely creating the **TrueCrypt** container file or virtual disk, inside which all your other encrypted data will be stored. Click on the **Next** button to continue.

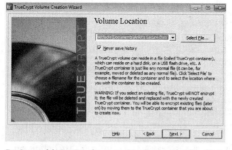

TrueCrypt and the TrueCrypt logo are registered trademarks of TrueCrypt Developers Association, used with permission.

TrueCrypt will now ask you to select the encryption algorithm which encrypts your file and the hash algorithm that encrypts your password. For most users, just selecting the default option is the way to go.

TrueCrypt and the TrueCrypt logo are registered trademarks of TrueCrypt Developers Association, used with permission.

In the next step, **TrueCrypt** will ask you to enter the size you wish to assign to the **TrueCrypt** container file (or virtual disk) that you are creating. Depending upon the size of the files you wish to encrypt and store, you need to specify an appropriate size. In this example, I've entered 100 MB as the size of the **TrueCrypt** container file (or virtual disk).

Now, you need to choose a password to secure the confidential data you will be storing. The longer the password, the better it is. The more complicated the password, the harder it will be to crack.

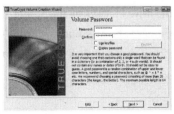

TrueCrypt and the TrueCrypt logo are registered trademarks of TrueCrypt Developers Association, used with permission.

In the next step, **TrueCrypt** will ask you to move your mouse around as randomly as possible within the application window. The more randomly you move your mouse and the longer you move it for, the stronger will be the encryption that **TrueCrypt** will use to encrypt your files. Click on the **Format** button whenever you are ready to create the **TrueCrypt** volume.

At this stage, you have successfully created the **TrueCrypt** volume (or virtual disk) where you will be able to save all your files securely in encrypted format. Click on the **Exit** button to end the **TrueCrypt Volume Creation Wizard**. You are now ready to start saving all your confidential files in encrypted format in the **TrueCrypt** virtual disk.

TrueCrypt and the TrueCrypt logo are registered trademarks of TrueCrypt Developers Association, used with permission.

Now, each time you wish to access (view, save, modify or delete) data stored in the **TrueCrypt** virtual disk, you need to mount it using the **TrueCrypt** app. Start **TrueCrypt** and select any drive letter you would like to mount your virtual disk as. In this example, I've selected the drive P:. Click on the **Select File** button, select the **TrueCrypt** container file (the one we created earlier) that you wish to mount as a virtual disk and click on the **Mount** button.

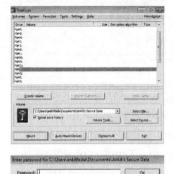

TrueCrypt will now ask you to enter the password you had chosen while creating the **TrueCrypt** volume. Without entering the correct password, no one can access any data stored in your **TrueCrypt** virtual disk. Click on the **OK** button to continue.

TrueCrypt and the TrueCrypt logo are registered trademarks of TrueCrypt Developers Association, used with permission.

TrueCrypt and the TrueCrypt logo are registered trademarks of TrueCrypt Developers Association, used with permission.

Within a few seconds, **TrueCrypt** will successfully mount the **TrueCrypt** volume as a virtual disk represented as P: on your system. You can now access all the files on this **TrueCrypt** encrypted virtual disk just the way you would access any other drive.

If you go to **My Computer** on your system, you will notice that a new drive P: has been mounted (notice that the size of the drive is approximately what we had selected—100 MB in this example). The moment you shut down your computer, or if your computer crashes, the mounted drive will disappear. It can be accessed by mounting the **TrueCrypt** virtual drive again, by selecting the container file and entering the correct password. Even if someone were to copy your container file and take it to another system, they will not be able to mount it and access your data without knowing your password.

TrueCrypt and the TrueCrypt logo are registered trademarks of TrueCrypt Developers Association, used with permission.

73. HOW TO IMPROVE THE SECURITY ON YOUR PHONE AND TABLET

 < 120 Seconds

The default security features on your devices are usually not adequate to give you proper security. If you would like to make it harder for anyone to illegally access the data on your Android device, it is important to customize the security settings on your device. It is highly recommended that every Android user follows the steps below to improve the security on their device:

1. Enable a strong screen lock password by going to **Settings > Location and security > Set screen lock**. It is recommended that you use an alphanumeric password instead of a numeric PIN or pattern as your password.

Android and the Android logo are registered trademarks of Google Inc., used with permission.

2. Enable the **Remote controls** option (Under **Settings** > **Location & Security**) on your Android device. This will allow you to remotely lock, trace and wipe data from your Android phone in case it is lost or stolen. Alternatively, you could install a third-party app like **Lookout** on your Android device.

Android and the Android logo are registered trademarks of Google Inc., used with permission.

3. It is advisable that you never install an app on your Android device that has not been downloaded from the official Android Market. Even while downloading an app from the official Android Market, make sure you read its reviews, check whether it is safe to use and confirm that other users did not face any security issues while using it. You can disable the installation of non-Market apps by going to **Settings** > **Application settings** and unselecting the **Unknown sources** option.

4. Switch off the wireless and Bluetooth functionality on your Android phone whenever you are not using them. This reduces the chances of unauthorized access to your device. To toggle the wireless and Bluetooth features on your device, go to **Settings** > **Wireless and network settings** and then select **Wi-Fi settings** or **Bluetooth settings** and change them on the basis of your preferences.

Android and the Android logo are registered trademarks of Google Inc., used with permission.

Android and the Android logo are registered trademarks of Google Inc., used with permission.

5. On certain Android versions you can encrypt all the contents of your phone and SD card so that none of the data stored on it can be accessed without entering an access password. To enable this encryption feature, simply press **Settings** > **Security** > **Encrypt** device.

6. Install an antivirus app on your mobile phone that will protect you against any infected files, malicious apps that you may download to your device and even SMS text message scams. For example, **AVG** is a free antivirus that does a great job of protecting your Android device. You can download it from **http://www.avg.com/in-en/antivirus-for-android**.

Once you enable these additional security features on your Android device, it drastically reduces the chances of someone else illegally accessing your device.

On an iOS device, a four-digit numeric password is used by default to unlock the screen. Although a four-digit password is easy to remember and convenient to quickly type in, from a security perspective it is not very secure. To improve the security of your iOS device, it is advisable to switch from the four-digit numeric password to a traditional alphanumeric password. Alphanumeric passwords are tougher to guess or find out. In order to do this, tap on **Settings** > **General** > **Passcode Lock**. Turn the **Simple Passcode** option off and enable the **Turn Passcode** On option. You will now be asked to enter a new alphanumeric password, which will be used in the future to unlock your screen.

1. It is also advisable to enable the **Erase Data** option on your iOS device, which will automatically erase all data from your device in case an incorrect unlock password is entered ten consecutive times. This additional security feature protects the confidential data on your iOS device from malicious users who are trying to guess your screen-unlock password. Moreover, if you enable this option, even if your iOS device gets stolen, at least the data on it will remain out of the hands of miscreants. To enable this option, go to **Settings** > **General** > **Passcode lock** and turn on **Erase Data**.

2. As with Android, switch off the Bluetooth and the Wi-Fi features on your iOS device by going to **Settings** and disabling them, whenever you are not using them. This reduces the chances of unauthorized access to your device.

3. It is a good idea to install the **Find My iPhone** app, available as a free download from the iTunes App store, so that it is easy to trace it in case it goes missing. This app not only shows you the exact geographical location of your missing device on a map, it also gives you the option to remotely wipe out all data from it. Moreover, **Find My iPhone** will allow you to play a loud alarm on your missing device to scare off potential thieves or to help you locate your missing device if you have dropped it in a dark room. Finally, this will app will also allow you to display a message on your missing device with your contact details.

Once you enable these additional security features on your iOS device, it significantly minimizes the chances of someone else illegally accessing your device and stealing data from it.

74. HOW TO PASSWORD-PROTECT APPS ON YOUR PHONE OR TABLET

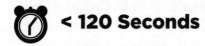 **< 120 Seconds**

A problem for many of us is how to protect our apps and data from friends, family and colleagues. If we share our device with someone and give them the phone-unlock password, they can also access the rest of the device. For these occasions, there is a way to password-protect our apps even if we use a device that we share with other people on occasion.

On your iOS device, go to **Settings** > **General** > **Restrictions**. By default the **Restrictions** setting will be off on your device. Simply tap on it to enable it.

Tap on the **Enable Restrictions** option to enable restrictions on access to specific apps on your device. You will now be asked to choose a password which will toggle whether restrictions on access to apps on your device is enabled or not. In other words, whenever the restrictions are enabled, the selected apps will not be displayed on your iOS device. To access any of the restricted apps, you have to disable the restrictions.

You can now choose which apps you would like to restrict or hide on your device. For example, you can disable the Safari browser, the camera on your device, the ability to install new apps, the ability to delete apps, iTunes etc.

To enable the restricted apps again, you need to tap **Settings** > **General** > **Restrictions**. You will be asked to enter the same password that you had selected in the earlier step. Tap on the **Disable Restrictions** option and you will be allowed to access all the restricted apps on your device.

Once you have enabled restrictions on your device, it is also possible to disable certain types of content on your iOS device. For example, you can disable TV shows, movies or music on your device, which may be inappropriate for your kids to access. It is also possible for you to disable access to all apps entirely.

Similarly, if you want to password-protect apps on your Android device, simply follow the steps below:

Go to the Google Play App Store, download and install the **Smart App Protector** app. It is available as a free download.

When you start **Smart App Protector** for the first time, you will be asked to enter the unlocking password, which is initially set to 7777 (you should obviously change this password). Enter the initial access password to continue.

Smart App Protector and the Smart App Protector logo are registered trademarks of SPSoft Mobile, used with permission.

When you press the **Add** button, all the installed apps on your

Android phone will be displayed on the screen. You can select which apps you would like to password-protect and restrict access to. In this example, I am going to password-protect Camera and Camera Zoom FX.

Smart App Protector and the Smart App Protector logo are registered trademarks of SPSoft Mobile, used with permission.

From now on, if anyone tries to launch any of the restricted apps, **Smart App Protector** will ask them to enter the access password. Without the correct password, none of the restricted apps will launch.

On the home screen of **Smart App Protector**, you can press the **Additional Locks** button to enable additional security features. Using this feature, you can disable the USB connection, outgoing calls, 3G data access, Wi-Fi and even the Manage Applications page on your phone.

75. HOW TO PASSWORD-PROTECT YOUR PHOTOS AND MOVIES ON IPHONES AND IPADS

 < 120 Seconds

If you have private photos on your iOS device and want to keep them completely private, it may be a good idea to password-

Private Photo Vault and the Private Photo Vault logo are registered trademarks of Enchanted Cloud Studios, used with permission.

protect them. There are various third-party apps available in the iTunes App store, which allow you to password-protect files on your iOS device. One of the most popular apps is **Private Photo Vault**.

Once you have installed **Private Photo Vault** on your iOS device, you need to choose a password that will protect all the confidential photos that you wish to hide on your device.

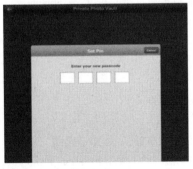

Private Photo Vault and the Private Photo Vault logo are registered trademarks of Enchanted Cloud Studios, used with permission.

Import all the confidential photos or videos from your device into **Private Photo Vault** by using the built-in interface. Any photo or video that you import into this app will be protected by the access password. Without entering the correct access password, no user will be allowed to view the protected photos and videos.

The interface of **Private Photo Vault** is very intuitive, user-friendly and easy to use. The process of importing photos, videos and other files into this app is a breeze. Once you have imported the files, make sure you manually delete the originals from the Camera Roll of your iOS device, since they will otherwise continue to be accessible there without a password.

76. HOW TO SECURE YOUR WI-FI NETWORK AT HOME

 < 120 Seconds

If you are worried about your neighbours misusing your home Wi-Fi network without permission, it is important that you take the necessary precautions to secure your Wi-Fi network. In order to achieve this, connect to your Wi-Fi network the way you normally do, click on the **Start** button and type 'cmd', and press enter to start the MS DOS prompt on your computer. In the MS DOS prompt type the following command:

ipconfig /all

Within the output screen, look for the **Wireless Network Connection**, and, under that, look for the IP address mentioned next to the **Default Gateway** entry. This is the address of your Wi-Fi router, using which you can connect to it. In the following example, the IP address of my Wi-Fi router is 192.168.0.1.

Start your browser and key in this IP address in the URL address

```
Wireless LAN adapter Wireless Network Connection:

   Connection-specific DNS Suffix  . :
   Link-local IPv6 Address . . . . . : fe80::9de:87be:ee89:544c%11
   IPv4 Address. . . . . . . . . . . : 192.168.0.100
   Subnet Mask . . . . . . . . . . . : 255.255.255.0
   Default Gateway . . . . . . . . . : 192.168.0.1
```

MS DOS is a registered trademark of Microsoft Inc., used with permission.

bar. This will allow you to connect to it and change its settings. Most Wi-Fi routers will ask you to enter a username and password to access the router settings page. Depending upon the manufacturer of your Wi-Fi router, the default username and password may vary. You can refer to your Wi-Fi router manual or the manufacturer's website to acquire the default password applicable to your router. For most routers, typing 'admin' as the username and 'admin' as the password, or typing 'admin' as the username and 'password' as the password should work.

Once you have successfully logged in, you will be allowed to change the settings related to your Wi-Fi network. Enable encryption on your Wi-Fi network, so that no one who doesn't have your access password is able to connect to your Wi-Fi, and, moreover, all your data communication is encrypted and secure. It is a good idea to enable WPA2 security on your Wi-Fi router instead of WEP or WPA security. As of now, WPA2 security with a strong password is the highest level of security available on a Wi-Fi network.

Wi-Fi Settings-->Security		
•Station List	•Basic	•Security
Security Policy		
Security Mode		WPA2-PSK
WPA		
WPA Algorithms		○ TKIP ● AES ○ AUTO
WPA Key		••••••••••••

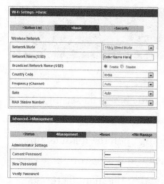

It is also advisable to change the name (also known as the SSID) of your Wi-Fi network to something that makes it harder for someone to figure out that the network belongs to you. Although changing the name of your network does not improve the security of your Wi-Fi network, you don't need to broadcast to everyone the fact that a particular network belongs to you. Moreover, using the default SSID name that was selected by your service provider tells the cybercriminal that you are not very tech-savvy, and attracts unnecessary attention. Just browse through your Wi-Fi router settings page to find the **SSID Network Name** option, and change it.

On the other hand, if you continue using the default username and password, any malicious user within the range of your Wi-Fi network will easily be able to access your router settings by typing its IP address in their browser. They can also change your security settings without your knowledge. Hence, it is highly recommended that you change your Wi-Fi router access password to prevent illegal access to it.

Besides, make sure you have disabled remote access and management of your Wi-Fi router settings, so that it cannot be remotely accessed.

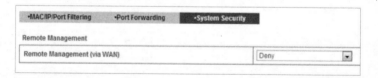

For advanced users, it is advisable that you enable **MAC Address Filtering** on your Wi-Fi router and manually enter the MAC addresses of all the devices (laptops, mobile phones, tablets and others) that you want to allow to connect to your Wi-Fi router.

Although **MAC Address Filtering** will keep most attackers away from your network, it is important to remember that a motivated cybercriminal can still use various techniques (e.g. MAC spoofing) to fool your Wi-Fi router. To prevent this, keep changing your Wi-Fi access password on a regular basis and make sure you choose strong passwords that are a combination of numbers, letters and symbols.

77. HOW TO TRACE YOUR LOST OR STOLEN MOBILE PHONE

 < 180 Seconds

Losing your mobile phone can be quite a painful ordeal. Not only does it burn a hole in your pocket, but it also causes a lot of inconvenience because of the loss of all your information. Whenever someone's phone gets lost or stolen, the first thing that comes to their mind is whether there is a way to trace it.

If you are using an Android or iOS-based smartphone, there is a wonderful app called **Lookout (http://www.lookout.com)** for just this purpose. It is available as a free download and, once installed on your phone, it can be of great help in case your mobile phone is stolen or lost. Just make sure that you have **Lookout** installed on your phone from before.

Lookout and the Lookout logo are registered trademarks of Lookout Inc., used with permission.

To start using **Lookout**, you need to download the app to your Android or iOS smartphone or tablet. In this example, I am going to install **Lookout** on my iPad. I have to create an account on the **Lookout** website to complete the installation process. Once I have installed **Lookout** on my device and created an account, my device is all set to be protected.

If this device gets lost or stolen, all you need to do is simply log in to your **Lookout** account from any computer. Once you log in, you will be taken to the **Lookout Dashboard**, which will allow you to trace your missing device with a single click of the mouse button. Typically, it doesn't take longer than a few minutes for **Lookout** to be able to find your device.

Lookout and the Lookout logo are registered trademarks of Lookout Inc., used with permission.

It is important to note that **Lookout** will be able to trace the geographical location of a missing device with much more accuracy if it is connected to a mobile phone network than if it is connected only to a Wi-Fi network. Using the **Lookout Dashboard**, not only can you trace your missing device, but you can also remotely erase all data from your missing device. This means that, even though you may have lost your device, your data on it cannot be accessed or misused. Finally, it is also possible for you to use the **Lookout Dashboard** to remotely set off a loud alarm on your missing device.

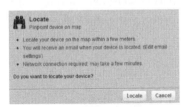

Lookout and the Lookout logo are registered trademarks of Lookout Inc., used with permission.

In this example, I am going to trace my missing iPad by clicking on the **Locate** button in my **Lookout Dashboard**. As we can see, **Lookout** has managed to trace my missing iPad, and has displayed its location as somewhere near the M-Block Market in Greater Kailash Part 2 in New Delhi.

Lookout and the Lookout logo are registered trademarks of Lookout Inc., used with permission.

78. HOW TO TRACE YOUR LOST OR STOLEN LAPTOP

 < 300 Seconds

If you are worried about losing your laptop or it getting stolen, it is time that you install a tracking software on it so that you can easily trace it back if it goes missing.

Prey is an open-source app that allows you to keep track of all your electronic devices (laptop, tablet and mobile phones). Once **Prey** has been installed on your laptop, it will silently run in the background and wait to receive a signal through the Internet from you. In case you have lost your laptop, you can log in to the web interface of **Prey** from anywhere in the world and send a signal to your laptop. Once the signal is received by the **Prey** software on your computer, it will allow you to perform the following actions, all remotely through the Internet and without physical access to your laptop:

1. Show the location of your device on a geographical map

2. Take a photo of the person using your device using the built-in camera

3. Lock down your computer, so that it cannot be used

4. Take a screenshot of your computer screen to find out more information about who is using your laptop. For example, you may be able to capture the email account or Facebook account that the user is logged into.

5. Set off a loud alarm on your missing laptop

6. Display an alert message on your laptop screen with the text of your choice

7. Erase all saved passwords and history from the browser on your missing device

After you have recorded the necessary information using **Prey**, you can try to find the missing laptop yourself or share this information with the police. It is important to note that you need to have installed **Prey** on your laptop before it goes missing. Download **Prey** on your laptop from **www.preyproject.com** and start the installation wizard. Make sure you select the **Configure Prey Settings** option in the last step. This will start the **Prey Configurator wizard**. Select the **New user** option and click **Next** to continue.

Prey and the Prey logo are registered trademarks of Fork Ltd, used with permission.

[Prey] Please activate your new account

Prey Control Panel <no-reply@preyproject.com>
to me

Hello Ankit Fadia from India!

Your account for Prey's Control Panel has been successfully created. However, to complete the signup process you need to activate it by clicking the following URL

http://panel.preyproject.com/activate/5a60466bd157475590573572615852415a3231666157777559323974a

If you haven't signed up for an account, please disregard this mail.

The Prey Team
http://preyproject.com

Enter your contact details and click on the **Create** button to create your **Prey** account and add your devices to it.

Prey and the Prey logo are registered trademarks of Fork Ltd, used with permission.

Log in to your email account to verify your identity by clicking on the link sent to you by the **Prey Project**.

Once you have verified your account, **Prey** will actively start tracking your laptop and allow you to trace it back in case it gets lost or stolen. You are now ready to log into your Web Control Panel to manage all the devices connected to your **Prey** account.

Prey and the Prey logo are registered trademarks of Fork Ltd, used with permission.

To manage the tracking settings related to a specific device, simply click on the device in the **Prey Control Panel**. This page will allow you specify what actions will be performed in case your device goes missing. Make the applicable changes and click on the **Save changes** button.

Prey and the Prey logo are registered trademarks of Fork Ltd, used with permission.

In case your device goes missing, simply log in to the **Prey Control Panel** from their website, select your device and change its status from **OK** to **MISSING**. After a few minutes, you will receive a detailed report about your missing device via email from the **Prey Project**.

This report will contain a bunch of information related to your missing device. The actions that are performed and things that are included in the report will depend upon the settings you had previously chosen in the **Control Panel**.

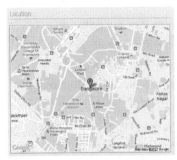

(Geographical Location of the Missing Laptop on a Map)　　*(Picture from the Webcam of the Missing Laptop)*

Prey and the Prey logo are registered trademarks of Fork Ltd, used with permission.

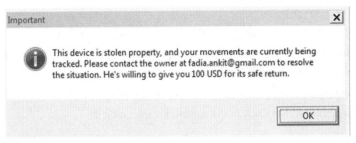

Prey and the Prey logo are registered trademarks of Fork Ltd, used with permission.

Locate My Laptop (www.locatemylaptop.com) is yet another website which allows you to remotely track your lost or stolen laptop. Moreover, it also allows you to remotely wipe all data from your missing laptop, if required.

Rewarding Return (www.rewardingreturn.com) is a website that allows you to purchase labels that you can put behind your electronic devices (laptops, digital cameras and mobile phones), so that if someone returns your device, they can collect a reward for it.

Every label has a unique ID number and the contact details of the **Rewarding Return** company printed on it, so that anyone who finds your electronic device knows how to contact them to return it.

If someone finds your electronic device, they can go to **www.rewardingreturn.com** or call them, quote the unique ID number and get rewarded for doing so. You can choose the reward amount initially when you purchase the **Rewarding Return** labels. In case you don't wish to give any cash reward, you can even choose to give free **Rewarding Return** labels to the finder. The **Rewarding Return** website will then arrange for your lost electronic device to be shipped back to you and will, on your behalf, reward the person who found it.

The limitation of the **Rewarding Return** website service is the fact that it depends entirely upon the goodness of the person who finds your device. This becomes especially limiting, since, on most occasions, the value of your missing device will usually be much higher than the value of the reward for returning it.

Using these several laptop-tracking techniques, even if your laptop goes missing, you still have the hope that it can be tracked and be recovered.

79. HOW TO USE YOUR MOBILE PHONE FOR YOUR PERSONAL SAFETY

 < 120 Seconds

Have you ever felt unsafe while travelling alone, and wished there was an automated way to notify your friends and family in case of an emergency? **StaySafe** is an Android and iOS app that allows you to automatically inform your emergency contacts and send them your latest GPS location, in case you don't check in to your app after a predefined time period. Just start the countdown on the app for a predefined amount of time, and, in case you don't cancel the countdown before it ends, **StaySafe** will automatically inform your emergency contacts. Unlike other location-sharing apps, **StaySafe** does not require any intervention from your side—so it is perfect to send out an alarm in case you get into some danger.

To use **StaySafe**, download the app to your mobile phone from the Google Play App Store or the iTunes app store.

Enter your name and contact number, so that your emergency contacts know your identity when they are informed that you may be in danger.

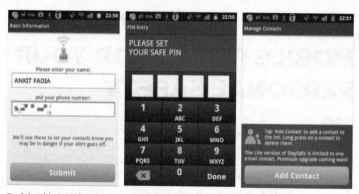

StaySafe and the StaySafe app logo are registered trademarks of Safe Apps Ltd, used with permission.

Choose a PIN or password for your **StaySafe account**. After that select the people from your address book whom you want **StaySafe** to inform in case of an emergency.

You are now ready to use **StaySafe** to inform your emergency contacts in case you are in danger. Whenever you start a journey on which you want **StaySafe** to look out for your safety, simply press the **Start Countdown** button. You will be asked to enter the duration of your journey, from which the app will start counting down. If required, you can increase the duration of your journey manually later; but if you do not cancel the countdown before it ends, **StaySafe** will automatically send your current location and inform all your emergency contacts that something is wrong.

StaySafe and the StaySafe app logo are registered trademarks of Safe Apps Ltd, used with permission.

StaySafe and the StaySafe app logo are registered trademarks of Safe Apps Ltd, used with permission.

Your emergency contacts will receive an email with a link to a web page that shows your current location and also the entire path you took since you started the countdown. In this example, the screen indicates that I'm in Sector 15, Pune, very close to the Dr D.Y. Patil Institute of Biotechnology.

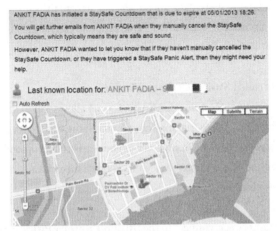

StaySafe and the StaySafe app logo are registered trademarks of Safe Apps Ltd, used with permission.

80. HOW TO TRACE A LOST OR STOLEN DIGITAL CAMERA

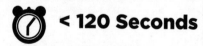 **< 120 Seconds**

Have you ever lost a digital camera while on holiday and wished there was a way to trace it back using some software or website? With the use of technology, there is greater hope and a more scientific way of tracking a lost or stolen digital camera.

Every photo that you take using a digital camera contains something called EXIF data that is stored with it. EXIF data, or Exchangeable Image File Format data, basically stores information like the camera manufacturer, model number, serial number, date and other details. Most modern cameras automatically store EXIF data in all photos taken with them. Every camera has a unique serial number, which is also stored in the EXIF data. All photos taken from the same camera will have the same serial number. This property can be used to track a stolen or lost digital camera.

A website called **Stolen Camera Finder (http://www.stolencamerafinder.com)** allows you to search the Internet for photos that may contain the same EXIF data (serial number) as yours. If the new owner of your camera has uploaded photos online, this website gives you a good chance of tracking down the camera through this.

Open your browser, connect to the **Stolen Camera Finder** website and upload a photo you have clicked with the missing camera in the past. It doesn't matter what photo it is or when you took it, as long as it was taken with the same camera as the one that is missing and has not been edited by some third-party app.

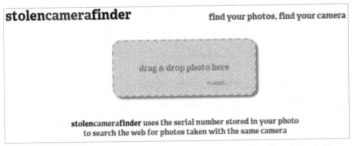

Stolen Camera Finder and the Stolen Camera Finder logo are registered trademarks of Matt Burns Ltd, used with permission.

Stolen Camera Finder does not actually store your photo, but it will extract the EXIF data from it and search the Internet for other photos with the matching EXIF data. If any match is found, it will report it to you so that you can take the action to get your camera back.

Stolen Camera Finder and the Stolen Camera Finder logo are registered trademarks of Matt Burns Ltd, used with permission.

In case you do not have any old photo taken with your missing camera, **Stolen Camera Finder** also allows you to manually enter

lost camera report

Stolen Camera Finder and the Stolen Camera Finder logo are registered trademarks of Matt Burns Ltd, used with permission.

the serial number of your camera, which is normally mentioned on the camera box which you received at the time of purchase. You can also click on the **Report stolen camera** or the **Report lost camera** button to file a report on this website, so that, in case someone else finds your camera, they can get in touch with you.

This website cannot guarantee that your camera will be found; however it does a good job of maximizing your chances in an age where everyone is constantly uploading photos online.

81. HOW TO SAVE YOUR PASSWORDS SECURELY

 < 180 Seconds

The number of activities that we do online has risen exponentially over time—email, social networking, banking, shopping, work, education etc. All of this requires usernames and passwords to access our information. For security reasons, it is recommended that you do not use the same password for different sites—if a malicious user figures out the password to one of your accounts, he will be able to access all your other accounts as well. The most secure way to store all your passwords to different accounts is to remember them, but, considering the large number of online accounts each of us has, this is very difficult. As a result, a lot of people end up saving all their passwords in a Notepad file or MS Word document on their computers. But, if you do that, your security comes under serious threat as soon as someone else shares your computer.

A much more secure alternative is to save your passwords in password managers. As the name suggests, password managers are tools that allow you to securely manage passwords to all your online accounts by saving them in a secure, encrypted format. All you need to remember is one master password, which will open up a virtual locker containing all your other passwords. Of the several password managers available on the Internet, my favourite is **KeePass**, which is available as a free download from **http://www.keepass.info**.

KeePass and the KeePass logo are registered trademarks of Dominik Reichl, used with permission.

Once you launch the **KeePass** app for the first time, you will need to click on the **New Password Database** button in the toolbar on the top. This will allow you to create a new database of saved passwords for yourself, inside which you will be able to save the passwords to all your different accounts.

KeePass will now ask you to enter a master password for all your saved passwords. The longer and more complicated your master password is, the more secure it is going to be—so choose wisely.

Once you have set a master password to the database, you can start adding password entries for your different accounts to it by clicking

KeePass and the KeePass logo are registered trademarks of Dominik Reichl, used with permission.

KeePass and the KeePass logo are registered trademarks of Dominik Reichl, used with permission.

on the **Add Entry** button in the toolbar. For each new password entry you add, you will be asked to enter various details (like **Title**, **Username**, **Password**, **URL**, **Expiry date** and **Group**). Click on the **OK** button to add the entry to your password database.

One of the best features of **KeePass** is that, when you are adding a new password entry, it will allow you to generate strong and difficult-to-crack passwords for your different accounts. By using the complex passwords that **KeePass** generates, you are going to make it tough for malicious users to be able to crack into your accounts. To access the **Password Generator** tool, simply click on the **Generate a Random Password** button within the **Add Entry** feature of **KeePass**.

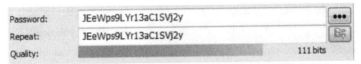

KeePass and the KeePass logo are registered trademarks of Dominik Reichl, used with permission.

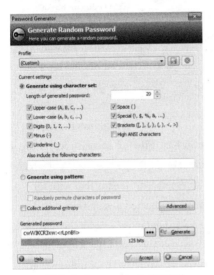

KeePass and the KeePass logo are registered trademarks of Dominik Reichl, used with permission.

The **Password Generator** tool allows you to choose the length, complexity and type of the random password you wish to generate. After selecting all the options of your choice, you need to simply click on the **Generate** button to generate a random password for your account. Once you are happy with the generated password, you can click on the **Accept** button to add it to the password database.

Another very useful feature in **KeePass** is the ability to put expiry dates on your passwords, so that it forces you to adopt the good habit of changing your passwords regularly. You can choose to automatically make your passwords expire at predefined intervals, ranging from one week to several months.

KeePass and the KeePass logo are registered trademarks of Dominik Reichl, used with permission.

Once you start using **KeePass**, you need to enter the master password into the app to access the saved passwords. However, for users who want an additional layer of security on their saved passwords, **KeePass** also allows the use of something known as a **Key File**. A **Key File** is a special encryption key that can be stored in a pen drive or a CD by a user, without which the saved passwords cannot be accessed. This means that without the pen drive or CD physically being connected to a system, it will be impossible to open the saved password database, even if the master password is entered correctly. To enable the use of the **Key File** facility along with the master password, you need to simply enable the **Use Master Password** and **Key File** option in **KeePass**.

Once you have added the passwords for all your different accounts to **KeePass**, it offers you various convenient options to log in to your accounts with these passwords. For this example, I am going to assume that you want to log in to your Facebook account using a password stored in **KeePass**.

Option 1
Open your browser > Connect to Facebook.com and type in your Username > Launch KeePass > Enter Master Password > Right-click on the Facebook Password entry > Select the Copy Password option > Paste it in the Password field on Facebook.com.

KeePass and the KeePass logo are registered trademarks of Dominik Reichl, used with permission.

Option 2

Open your browser > Connect to Facebook.com and type your Username > Click in the Password field on Facebook.com > Launch KeePass > Enter Master Password > Right-click on the Facebook Password entry > Select the Perform Auto Type option and the password will automatically be typed in the selected field in your browser.

If you use multiple computers to access your accounts, I would recommend downloading the portable version of **KeePass**. This portable version can be taken in a pen drive with you wherever you go, along with your saved passwords and key file, and can be run directly without any installation.

Some other similar programs are:

▶ **Clipperz**
▶ **LastPass**

82. HOW TO TRACE AN EMAIL BACK TO THE INTERNET SERVICE PROVIDER

 **< 180 Seconds**

Have you ever received an unpleasant email sent from a fake email account created by supplying false contact information? Do not worry, it is possible for you to trace the email back and find out the IP address, location (city and country) and Internet Service Provider (ISP) of the sender. You might be able to deduce the identity of the sender with this information.

```
Delivered-To: fadia.ankit@gmail.com
Received: by 10.182.52.200 with SMTP id v8csp19069lcbc;
    Sat, 20 Oct 2012 01:13:00 -0700 (PDT)
Received: by 10.60.20.41 with SMTP id k9mr10696oee.39.1350720780145;
    Sat, 20 Oct 2012 01:13:00 -0700 (PDT)
Return-Path: <bouncy@spypig.com>
Received: from ube.ubergreed.com (ube.ubergreed.com. [96.125.172.16])
    by mx.google.com with ESMTPS id ab5si3999977obc.98.2012.10.20.01.12.59
    (version=TLSv1/SSLv3 cipher=OTHER);
    Sat, 20 Oct 2012 01:13:00 -0700 (PDT)
Received-SPF: pass (google.com: domain of bouncy@spypig.com designates 96.125.172
Authentication-Results: mx.google.com; spf=pass (google.com: domain of bouncy@spy
Received: from uber by ube.ubergreed.com with local (Exim 4.77)
    (envelope-from <bouncy@spypig.com>)
    id 1TFUB1-0001Ke-Iw
    for fadia.ankit@gmail.com; Sat, 20 Oct 2012 08:12:59 +0000
To: <fadia.ankit@gmail.com>
Subject: Your email "Bareilly" has been read 1 time!
X-PHP-Script: www.spypig.com/pig.php for 220.225.12.210
MIME-Version: 1.0
Content-type: text/html; charset=iso-8859-1
From: SpyPig Notification <oink@spypig.com>
Reply-To: SpyPig <oink@spypig.com>
Message-Id: <E1TFUB1-0001Ke-Iw@ube.ubergreed.com>
Date: Sat, 20 Oct 2012 08:12:59 +0000
X-AntiAbuse: This header was added to track abuse, please include it with any abu
X-AntiAbuse: Primary Hostname - ube.ubergreed.com
X-AntiAbuse: Original Domain - gmail.com
```

To trace an email back to its sender, begin with opening the headers of the email that you wish to trace back. If you are using Gmail, open the email, click on the down arrow button located in the top right corner of the screen, and then click on the **Show Original** option to view the email headers. If you are using Yahoo, simply open the email, click on **Settings** and **Full Header**. If you are using an email client, right-click on the email and click on **Properties**, to view the email headers.

Now download the **eMailTrackerPro** application from **www.emailtrackerpro.com**, so that you can analyse the email headers and trace them back to the sender. Copy-paste the email headers to **eMailTrackerPro** and it will trace the email back to the sender and show you much other information about the sender. In the following example, **eMailTrackerPro** has displayed the sender's IP address, geographical location on a world map and also his ISP network information.

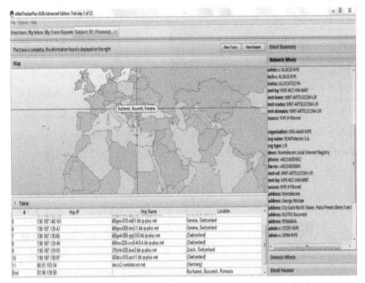

emailTrackerPro and the emailTrackerPro logo are registered trademarks of Visualware Inc., used with permission.

83. HOW TO TRACE YOUR LOST OR STOLEN ANDROID PHONE

 < 120 Seconds

In an earlier tip, we saw how easy it is to install the Lookout app on your mobile phone, so that you can trace it back in case it gets lost or stolen. However, how do you trace an Android mobile device that has already been lost or stolen and does not have a tracking software installed on it? Fortunately, for Android users only, there is a wonderful app called **Plan B** which allows you to trace a missing mobile phone by itself.

Plan B and the Plan B logo are registered trademarks of Lookout Inc., used with permission.

As soon as you discover that your Android phone is missing, use any computer to go to the Google Play App Store and download and install **Plan B**. Make sure you are logged in to the same Google account that you normally use to download apps on your missing Android phone.

Plan B and the Plan B logo are registered trademarks of Lookout Inc., used with permission.

Google Play will now ask you whether you wish to remotely send the **Plan B** app to your lost Android phone. Make sure the correct phone model and network provider are mentioned on the screen. Click on the **Install** button to continue.

Plan B and the Plan B logo are registered trademarks of Lookout Inc., used with permission.

The great part about **Plan B** is that you don't require physical access to the missing device to remotely install the program on it. Moreover, during installation, no prompt will show up on the screen of your missing phone either. It is only on your computer that you will see a confirmation message, saying **Plan B** will soon be downloaded to your missing mobile phone.

Plan B and the Plan B logo are registered trademarks of Lookout Inc., used with permission.

If **Plan B** manages to connect to your phone, you will soon receive an email at your Gmail account, containing a map with the exact location of your phone pinpointed. Now, all you need to do is to physically retrieve the phone for yourself.

84. HOW TO BLOCK INAPPROPRIATE WEBSITES AND CONTENT FROM YOUR KIDS

 < 420 Seconds

Are you worried about your kids visiting websites they shouldn't be? It is obviously not possible to constantly monitor everything that your kids do on the Internet. However, there are some simple things that you can do on your computer to block websites with objectionable content and prevent your kids from accessing them.

If there are specific websites that you want to block, you can access a specific file called 'hosts' in your Windows computer. To open the 'hosts' file on your computer, make sure you are logged in as the administrator, then launch the Notepad app, click on **File** > **Open** and open the following location: **C:\Windows\system32\drivers\etc\hosts.**

```
hosts - Notepad
File  Edit  Format  View  Help
# Copyright (c) 1993-2009 Microsoft Corp.
#
# This is a sample HOSTS file used by Microsoft TCP/IP for Windows.
#
# This file contains the mappings of IP addresses to host names. Each
# entry should be kept on an individual line. The IP address should
# be placed in the first column followed by the corresponding host name.
# The IP address and the host name should be separated by at least one
# space.
#
# Additionally, comments (such as these) may be inserted on individual
# lines or following the machine name denoted by a '#' symbol.
#
# For example:
#
#      102.54.94.97     rhino.acme.com          # source server
#       38.25.63.10     x.acme.com              # x client host

# localhost name resolution is handled within DNS itself.
#       127.0.0.1       localhost
#       ::1             localhost
```

Go to a new line at the bottom of the file and enter the following
text:

127.0.0.1 www.WebsiteToBlock.com
127.0.0.1 www.AnotherWebsiteToBlock.com

For example, if you want to block Facebook, you need to type the
following into the hosts file:

127.0.0.1 www.facebook.com

Although this blocking technique is quite effective, it has its own
limitations. For example, it is quite difficult for you to manually
block each of the possible inappropriate websites that you don't
want your kids to access. For more comprehensive protection, I
would recommend professional parental control software like
Net Nanny (www.netnanny.com).

Although **Net Nanny** is not free, it comes with a comprehensive list
of built-in security and safety measures that will protect your kids
from inappropriate websites and content on the Internet, including:

1. Blocking pornography
2. Blocking vulgar and profane language
3. Monitoring your kids' interactions on social media websites like Facebook and chat softwares
4. Implementing restrictions on how much and for how long your kids can use the Internet.

It is also recommended that you enable the **SafeSearch** filter on Google, which prevents explicit and inappropriate content from showing up in the Google Search results when your kids are searching for something. To enable this, log in to a Google account using the computer that your kids usually use and then go to **http://www.google.com/preferences** and then enable the **Filter explicit results** option.

Safe Search filters

Turn on SafeSearch to filter sexually explicit content from your search results.

☐ Filter explicit results.   Lock SafeSearch

Google SafeSearch and the Google logo are the registered trademarks of Google Inc.,used with permission

To prevent anyone from being able to disable the **SafeSearch** filter, you should click on the **Lock SafeSearch** option.

With these simple solutions, you can prevent your kids from being able to access inappropriate content and websites on the Internet.

FUN STU FF!

85. HOW TO CONVERT YOUR COMPUTER INTO A PHOTO BOOTH

 < 60 Seconds

Photo booths are normally found in shopping malls, airports and office complexes, and have automatic cameras that can take a series of fun photos you and your friends. Before taking each photo, the photo booth displays a flash notification or countdown, informing you that a photo is going to be taken, so that you can prepare to pose. Photo booths can be a lot of fun, since they allow you to add funky special effects to all the photos that you take there. Typically, these booths require a credit card or cash to operate. Why pay for using photo booths, when you could convert the webcam in your computer into a photo booth for free?

Webcam Toy and the Webcam Toy logo are registered trademarks of Neave Interactive Ltd, used with permission.

Webcam Toy (http://webcamtoy.com) is a free website that allows you to take photo-booth quality pictures and add more than seventy special effects and filters to them right from the webcam on your computer! To start using this website, open your browser to **www.webcamtoy.com** and click on the **Ready? Smile!** button. **Webcam Toy** will ask for your permission to access the webcam on your computer. Click on the **Use my camera!** button to continue.

Webcam Toy and the Webcam Toy logo are registered trademarks of Neave Interactive Ltd, used with permission.

Choose from any of the over seventy different special effects and filters available on this website. Make sure that you and your friends have struck a pose in front of your webcam, and then click on the **Camera** button. The app will do a countdown from 3 to 1, click a picture from your webcam, and then automatically add to it the special effects that you chose.

After that, you will have the option to either save the photo on your computer or instantly share it with your friends using Twitter or Facebook.

86. HOW TO DISCOVER NEW MUSIC BY CREATING PLAYLISTS IN YOUTUBE

 < 180 Seconds

Listening to good music can really relax the body, mind and soul. And, if you are like me, being able to listen to music free of cost probably relaxes you even more. YouTube.com is one of the most popular websites that allows you to listen to music free of cost. However, the biggest problem with YouTube is that you can't really create a playlist—the moment a video stops playing, you have to interrupt your work, go to the YouTube window and select the next video to play.

This is where YouTube's **Music Discovery Project** comes into the picture. This feature of YouTube can accessed at **http://www.youtube. com/disco**, and allows you to create playlists of songs of your favourite artist, so that there is no interruption in your musical experience. Simply open this web page and type in the name of any artist in the space provided. In this example, I am going to type 'DJ Tiesto' and then click on the **Disco!** button.

YouTube Music Discovery and the YouTube Music Discovery logo are registered trademarks of YouTube LLC, used with permission.

YouTube will now automatically create me a playlist containing the top songs of DJ Tiesto. Instead of choosing a specific artist, you can also click on the **Play top 100** link to create a playlist containing the hundred most popular songs from YouTube.

Once you start playing the videos, there will be a playlist navigation bar below the video, which gives you full control over various aspects of the playlist. You can easily switch to a specific song of your choice from anywhere in the playlist with a single click of the mouse button. You can even choose to switch on the **Shuffle** option.

This YouTube feature gives you the power of an uninterrupted musical experience, and also helps you discover new songs and artists.

87. HOW TO CONTROL MUSIC ON YOUR PHONE WITH A WAVE OF YOUR HAND

 < 120 Seconds

Have you been in a situation where your hands were dirty or you were holding something in both hands, and you couldn't change the song you were listening to on your phone? For these times, wouldn't it be great if there was a way to control the music playback on your mobile phone without having to actually touch the phone?

Wave Control is a free app available for both Android and iPhone devices that allows you to control the music playback functions on your phone by simply waving your hands in front of the screen. It makes use of the proximity sensor in your mobile phone (usually located next to the earpiece) to control various media functions on your phone. With **Wave Control**, you can simply wave your hand in certain specific gestures to control various playback options related to music or video on your phone.

Download, install and launch the **Wave Control** app on your Android or iPhone device. On the home screen, you will be able to manage the configuration settings related to your mobile phone. For example, you can choose to start **Wave Control** automatically whenever any other media app is launched You can also choose to exit the app automatically as soon as the headphones are unplugged from your mobile phone. In this example, I have selected to start

Wave Control automatically whenever I start the Poweramp app.

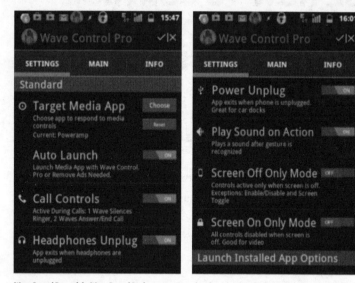

Wave Control Pro and the Wave Control Pro logo are registered trademarks of MarksThinkTank, used with permission.

Press the **MAIN** tab to link specific media functions to specific hand gestures made in front of the mobile phone screen. In this example, I have configured the following hand-wave gesture functions:

Hand Wave Gesture	Function
Hover	Play / Pause
1 Wave	Next song or video
2 Waves	Previous song or video
3 Waves	Enable/Disable control

A more advanced version of **Wave Control** is called **Wave Control Pro,** which comes for a nominal fee. Let us now put **Wave Control Pro** to test. Imagine that my hands are occupied and I am listening to music in Poweramp on my Android phone. I want to control the music functions in Poweramp without touching my mobile phone. I try these following pre-configured hand-wave gestures in front of the mobile screen:

Wave Control Pro and the Wave Control Pro logo are registered trademarks of MarksThinkTank, used with permission.

1. No Hand Gesture

Wave Control Pro: No Last Action.

Poweramp: The song 'Cocktail' is not playing.

Wave Control Pro and the Wave Control Pro logo are registered trademarks of MarksThinkTank, used with permission.

2. After Hover Hand Gesture

Wave Control Pro: Last Action recorded is Play/Pause.

Poweramp: The song 'Cocktail' has started playing.

Wave Control Pro and the Wave Control Pro logo are registered trademarks of MarksThinkTank, used with permission.

The best thing about **Wave Control** on Android is the fact that you can run it in the background, lock your screen, and the hand-wave gestures will still work. **Wave Control** works almost in the same manner on an iPhone—the only difference being that the **Wave Control** app must be open and the screen should be switched on. There are more configuration options available on Android as compared to the iPhone.

88. HOW TO CONVERT YOUR PHONE INTO A REMOTE CONTROL FOR YOUR COMPUTER

 < 300 Seconds

Have you ever wanted to remotely control your computer from your mobile phone, so that you don't need to take the trouble of going close to it? Imagine you are hosting a party at home and want to be able to mingle with the guests, while simultaneously playing DJ and controlling the music playing from your laptop. You could do this if you have the **Unified Remote** app.

Unified Remote and the Unified Remote logo are registered trademarks of Unified Intents AB, used with permission.

Unified Remote comes in two parts—the **Unified Remote** server that needs to be installed on the computer you wish to remotely control, and the **Unified Remote** app that needs to be installed on your Android phone. First, install the **Unified Remote** server from **http://www.unifiedremote.com** on your computer and make sure that the Windows firewall is not blocking it. Once you have installed the server on your computer, you should download and install **Unified Remote** from the Google Play App Store on your Android phone.

Unified Remote and the Unified Remote logo are registered trademarks of Unified Intents AB, used with permission.

As soon as you launch **Unified Remote** on your Android phone, it will ask you whether you want it to automatically scan for the corresponding **Unified Remote** server or whether you want to add it manually. I recommend that you manually add the server.

If your computer is connected to the Internet through a router, you need to enable **Port Forwarding** on it so that **Unified Remote** on your Android phone is able to connect to your computer. My computer is connected to the Internet through a Wi-Fi router, so I use the browser on my computer to connect to my Wi-Fi router and change its settings to enable **Port Forwarding**. You can get detailed instructions on how to enable **Port Forwarding** on your Wi-Fi router by visiting **www.portforward.com**.

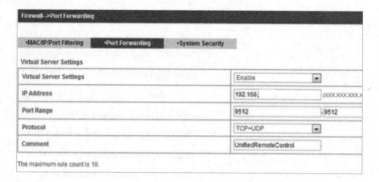

The key thing to remember is to enter the following values when you are enabling port forwarding on your Wi-Fi router:

Unified Remote and the Unified Remote logo are registered trademarks of Unified Intents AB, used with permission.

1. IP Address

In this field you need to enter the private IP address of your computer. To find this, you need to open **Unified Remote** server on your computer > Click on the **Connection** tab > Click on the **Network Interfaces** button, and usually the IP address mentioned in the first entry is what you need.

2. Port Range

From Port 9512 to Port 9512

3.Protocol

TCP and UDP

Manually adding the server to **Unified Remote** is not too complicated. In the **Host IP / Address** field, you need to enter the external public IP address of the computer you want to control from your Android phone. To find the external IP address of your computer, start your browser on it and connect to the website **What Is My IP Address (www.whatismyipaddress.com)**.

Unified Remote and the Unified Remote logo are registered trademarks of Unified Intents AB, used with permission.

Whatever IP address is displayed by the website is the external IP address of your computer. Enter it in the **Host / IP Address** field in **Unified Remote** on your phone. All the other fields will be pre-filled by **Unified Remote** and you don't need to make any changes to them. Tap the **Save** button to continue.

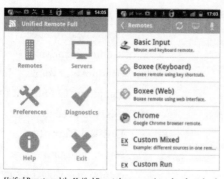

Unified Remote and the Unified Remote logo are registered trademarks of Unified Intents AB, used with permission.

Unified Remote will now connect to your computer and allow you to remotely control stuff on it through the Internet. To check whether you have successfully connected to your computer and troubleshoot connection issues, you need to tap the **Diagnostics** option on the **Unified Remote** dashboard screen.

To start controlling your computer, go into **Remotes** section of **Unified Remote**. There is a variety of controls available, each of which allows you to remotely control or perform a number of different tasks on your computer.

Some of my favourite and most useful remote controls are these:

1. Basic Input

Using this remote control, you can control the mouse on your computer and type stuff on your computer.

Unified Remote and the Unified Remote logo are registered trademarks of Unified Intents AB, used with permission.

Unified Remote and the Unified Remote logo are registered trademarks of Unified Intents AB, used with permission.

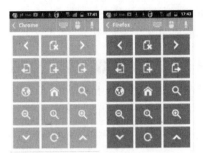

2. Chrome and Firefox

Using these remote controls you can control all aspects of your favourite browser on your computer, including opening a new tab, browsing to a particular website, closing a tab, moving between tabs,

Unified Remote and the Unified Remote logo are registered trademarks of Unified Intents AB, used with permission.

going to the home page, refreshing a page, scrolling up and down, zooming in to a page and so on.

3. File Manager

As the name suggests, this remote control allows you to navigate through all the files on your computer remotely. Moreover, you can remotely carry out various functions on your files, like open, delete, move, cut, copy and so on. This can also be used to launch apps on your computer by browsing to their folders.

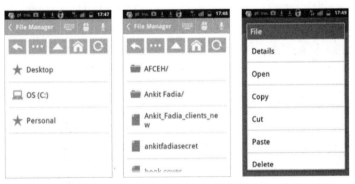

Unified Remote and the Unified Remote logo are registered trademarks of Unified Intents AB, used with permission.

4. Custom Run and Custom Windows

These remote controls allow you to launch apps on your computer and implement Windows shortcuts on them, like minimize, maximize and others. It is probably one of the best ways to launch apps on your computer from your phone.

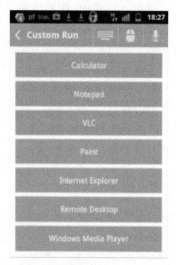 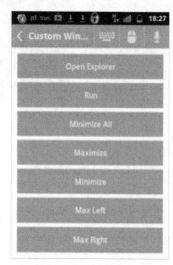

Unified Remote and the Unified Remote logo are registered trademarks of Unified Intents AB, used with permission.

5. Power

These remote controls allow you to remotely shut down, restart, hibernate or log out of your computer or even resume it if it is switched off. Perfect for playing pranks on your friends!

6. iTunes

Using the iTunes remote control from your Android phone, you can launch the

Unified Remote and the Unified Remote logo are registered trademarks of Unified Intents AB, used with permission.

iTunes app on your computer and control all the music that is playing on it. Similarly, **Unified Remote** also has remote controls that allow you to control other media apps on

Unified Remote and the Unified Remote logo are registered trademarks of Unified Intents AB, used with permission.

your computer, including Windows Media Player, VLC, Winamp, Spotify, Pandora, Netflix, Hulu and others.

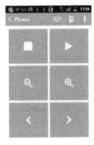

7. Picasa

This remote control is perfect if you have people over and want to show photos to them on a big screen (like your TV screen or even your room wall!), and want to control the flow of your Picasa photos remotely from your Android phone.

Unified Remote and the Unified Remote logo are registered trademarks of Unified Intents AB, used with permission.

8. PowerPoint Basic and PowerPoint Advanced

If you are giving a presentation and want to remotely control the flow of your presentation slides from your Android phone, these are the remote controls you need. The only limitation is that you need to first launch PowerPoint on your computer, and only then will this remote control become active.

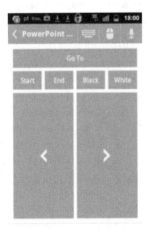

Unified Remote and the Unified Remote logo are registered trademarks of Unified Intents AB, used with permission.

Unified Remote and the Unified Remote logo are registered trademarks of Unified Intents AB, used with permission.

Unified Remote and the Unified Remote logo are registered trademarks of Unified Intents AB, used with permission.

9. Start

You can use this to launch apps that are listed in the Start menu of your computer.

10. YouTube

This remote control allows you to remotely manage the media controls for videos that you are watching on YouTube using your computer. For this remote control to work, you need to make sure that the focus is currently on YouTube on your computer—otherwise it doesn't work.

To prevent cybercriminals from connecting to your computer for malicious purposes, it is highly recommended that you enable an access password on the **Unified Remote** server. To password-protect the **Unified Remote** server on your computer, simply start the app and go to **Security** tab and select the **Enable password protection** option on it.

Unified Remote and the Unified Remote logo are registered trademarks of Unified Intents AB, used with permission.

Unified Remote and the Unified Remote logo are registered trademarks of Unified Intents AB, used with permission.

Once you have enabled password protection on the **Unified Remote** server, the next time you try to connect to your computer from your Android phone, you will need to enter the access password by going to the **Unified Remote** dashboard > **Servers** > **selecting your server** > entering the access password in the **Password** field.

With the help of **Unified Remote** you can control everything on your computer almost as if you were sitting in front of it!

89. HOW TO MAKE BASIC CONVERSATION IN FOREIGN LANGUAGES USING YOUR MOBILE PHONE

 < 60 Seconds

Imagine that you are lost in a foreign country where no one speaks English and all attempts to communicate with the locals in broken English or exaggerated gestures also fail. Do not worry—you can communicate with non-English speakers with the help of **Google Translate** on your mobile phone.

*Google Translate and the Google Translate logo are
registered trademarks of Google Inc., used with permission.*

*Google Translate and the Google Translate logo are
registered trademarks of Google Inc., used with permission.*

**Google Translate
(http://translate.google.
com)** is a free app that
translates text from one
language to another and can
also read it out aloud, using
the built-in speaker on your
phone. To use this app, open
the browser on your phone or
tablet to **Google Translate**
and type in whatever text you
wish to translate. You can
type in English or in any other
supported language.

From the drop-down list, select the language into which you wish to
translate the input text and press the **Go** button. In this example, I
am going to select Spanish as the final language. As of now, **Google
Translate** supports more than sixty five languages.

*Google Translate and the Google Translate logo are
registered trademarks of Google Inc., used with permission.*

After I enter my input text,
Google Translate will
translate it from English to
Spanish, and display it on
the screen. You can either
show the translated text to
the Spanish speaker, or you can press the **Speak** button and let
Google Translate read out the translated text aloud for you. Even
though the translation done by this tool will be a little textbookish
and may not always be perfect, it will at least help you get by in case
you are lost in a foreign land.

90. HOW TO USE THE PANIC BUTTON TO HIDE STUFF FROM YOUR BOSS

 < 60 Seconds

Imagine that you are in the office, and watching some videos on YouTube instead of doing your work. Even if you have a cool boss, you don't want him to get the impression that you are slacking off work. Since bosses often like to prowl around unannounced, you won't have the time to close all the open tabs in your browser, once you are chanced upon. The best you can do is minimize your browser and hope that your boss simply keeps walking and doesn't linger at your desk for too long. However, a bunch of minimized browser windows is visible even from a distance, and is a sure sign of no productive work being done.

Panic Button and the Panic Button logo are registered trademarks of Privax Ltd, used with permission.

Don't worry, because there is a panic-button app that can be installed in your browser, which will not only minimize all your open tabs but also open a safe, work-related website instantly. It is available as a free download for both Google Chrome and Mozilla Firefox.

Once it is installed, **Panic Button** will add an actual panic button next to the URL address bar of your browser. Right-click on it and select **Options** to manage the settings of this app.

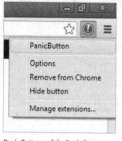

On the **Settings** page of **Panic Button**, you can completely customize its behaviour and working to suit your preferences. Normally, you need to click the panic button in the browser address bar to hide all open tabs. However, the **Settings** page of this app will also allow you to set up a keyboard shortcut that will do the same thing much faster. Whenever

Panic Button and the Panic Button logo are registered trademarks of Privax Ltd, used with permission.

you see your boss walking towards your desk, simply press the keyboard shortcut to hide all the open tabs in your browser!

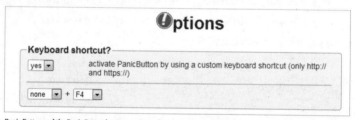

Panic Button and the Panic Button logo are registered trademarks of Privax Ltd, used with permission.

The best part about **Panic Button** is that you can set it up in such a way that it will also open a safe page instead of your already open tabs. You can also choose to hide the **Panic Button** icon from your toolbar once it has been activated.

Once it is safe to go back to your open tabs, you can reopen all the hidden tabs with a single click of the mouse on Panic Button. The **Settings** page also allows you to set a password to protect the saved hidden tabs from prying eyes. In other words, without entering the password, nobody will be able to reopen the saved hidden tabs on your browser. This is an additional safety feature in case someone else accesses your computer and browser.

91. HOW TO ACCESS BLOCKED WEBSITES

 **< 120 Seconds**

Internet censorship has become all-encompassing in the past few years. Most governments, companies and even colleges block access to popular websites like Facebook, YouTube and others.

In order to understand how to unblock access to these blocked websites, it is important to understand how your local network administrator blocks access. Typically, all networks will maintain a list or a database of blocked websites. Whenever you type a website address in your browser, that address is compared with the list of blocked websites. If what you typed in your browser is found in the blocked list, then you are blocked and shown an 'access denied' error message. On the other hand, if what you type in your browser does not appear in the blocked list, you will be given access to it. This is where something known a proxy server comes into play.

A proxy server is a means to indirectly access a website with the help of a browser to conceal the location of the user. It accepts the request for a specific web page, processes the request, fetches the required web page and displays it immediately back to the user. The firewall or filtering mechanism on the local network of the user thinks that the user is merely connecting to the web proxy—which in itself is not blocked—but the address of the blocked website is not registered. In other words, a proxy server is a way to bypass filters and gain access to blocked websites on the Internet.

Web proxy servers not only allow you to bypass blocking censors, they also protect your IP address or identity, giving you complete anonymity on the Internet. Proxy servers act as a mask for you as you surf the Internet. One of the most popular proxy servers on the Internet is a website called **Anonymizer (http://www.anonymizer.ru)**, which allows you anonymous access to blocked websites on the Internet.

As the name suggests, this is a Russian website. There are a lot of practical advantages of using Russian websites. Most Russian websites are free and, more importantly, most of them are completely anonymous and do not maintain any records of their users' activities.

Once you have connected to **Anonymizer**, type in the address of the website you need in the space provided on the top right corner of the screen, and click on whatever looks like the '**submit**' button.

For example, if you type http://www.google.com. **Anonymizer** will connect to the Google website, fetch the web page and display it on your screen, Google will record that someone from Russia is connecting to it, but not your IP address. From the other side, your local network administrator will record that you are merely connecting to the **Anonymizer** website, and not to Google.

If you use **Anonymizer** from **www.anonymizer.com** and **www. anonymizer.ru** frequently enough, sooner or later your network administrator will block them as well. But the good news is that there are thousands of such web proxies available on the Internet. Some of the most popular and reliable ones are the following:

- **http://www.hidemyass.com**
- **http://www.cooltunnel.com**
- **http://www.bypassthat.com**
- **http://www.btunnel.com**
- **http://ztunnel.com**
- **http://anonymouse.org**
- **http://thexite.com**
- **http://getus.in**
- **http://anonsurf.org**

92. HOW TO RECOGNIZE A SONG PLAYING SOMEWHERE

 < 180 Seconds

Has it ever happened that you are at some place and hear a song playing you really like, but have no clue which song it is? It happens to me all the time—at a bar or club, listening to the radio in the car, at the shopping mall or while watching TV in a friend's house. There is no longer any need to keep trying to guess which song is playing, instead just **Shazam** it!

Shazam (http://www.shazam.com) is an app that you can download on most mobile and tablet platforms. It is able to identify any song by recording the music playing in the background and comparing it to its growing database of approximately ten million songs. The most impressive thing about **Shazam** is that it doesn't matter what part of the song is playing when you run it, it will still identify the song! The only thing it requires to work properly is Internet access on that mobile phone. In this example, I am going to run **Shazam** on my iPad.

This is the **Shazam** app home screen. In the left column, **Shazam** displays the top most tagged (or **Shazam**-ed) songs currently in the world. To view all the songs that you have **Shazam**-ed until now, you need to press the **My Tags** button.

Shazam and the Shazam logo are registered trademarks of Shazam Entertainment Ltd, used with permission.

To identify a song that is playing somewhere, you need to press the **Shazam** button on the top right corner of the app. Make sure that you are as close as possible to the source of the music, and avoid covering the microphone of your device with your hands while running **Shazam**.

Shazam will now listen to the song playing in the background, compare it with all songs in its

Shazam and the Shazam logo are registered trademarks of Shazam Entertainment Ltd, used with permission.

database, and try to identify the song. The whole process does not take more than a few seconds.

As soon as it identifies the song, **Shazam** will display various details related to it. In this case, the song turns out be 'Beautiful Life' by the Shawn Anthony Band, featuring Aqua, and the album is *Beautiful Life*.

Using the **Similar** feature in the right column of Shazam, you can discover other songs that are similar to the song that has been identified. This is a great way to discover new music that you would otherwise not come across.

Moreover, **Shazam** is completely integrated with popular social networking platforms and allows users to not only share tagged songs with friends, but also watch the music video of a tagged song on YouTube. If the song is available on iTunes, **Shazam** will also show you the option to buy it from the iTunes store.

Shazam will usually recognize most English songs. It also often recognizes popular songs in other languages. To test the versatility of **Shazam's** database of songs, I decided to try to confuse the app by playing the song 'Ya Ali' from the Bollywood movie *Gangster*, which is supposedly inspired from the Arabic song 'Ya Ghaly' by Guitara. I tried this multiple times with different portions of both songs, and each time **Shazam** recognized which song I was playing!

93. HOW TO CREATE A DISPOSABLE EMAIL ACCOUNT

 < 120 Seconds

A disposable email address is a temporary email address that automatically expires after a predefined period of time. They are usually created so that they can be given to websites, individuals and companies that you don't necessarily trust and suspect of wanting to send you spam. They are also useful in situations where you want to receive emails from someone without revealing your true identity to them.

Anonymous Email and the Anonymous Email logo are registered trademarks of Privax Ltd, used with permission

To create a disposable email account for yourself, start your browser and connect to the **Anonymous Email** feature on the **HideMyAss** website **(http://www.hidemyass. com/anonymous-email/)**. Fill out the form to create a disposable email account for yourself, which in this case will come with the extension @hmamail.com. You can choose any username and password you want for the disposable email account, like you do when you create any other email account. The difference lies in the fact that you also need to specify an expiry date for your disposable email account, on which it will self-destruct automatically. The expiry date can be anything from twenty-four hours to a year. Finally, you can also specify your real email address, where you will receive notifications whenever you get a new email in your disposable account.

To log in to your disposable email account, open your browser to **Anonymous Email** whenever you want.

Anonymous Email and the Anonymous Email logo are registered trademarks of Privax Ltd, used with permission

Some other popular disposable email account providers are the following:

- Guerrilla Mail (www.guerrillamail.com)
- Fake Inbox (www.fakeinbox.com)
- Spamex (www.spamex.com)
- Mailinator (www.mailinator.com)

94. HOW TO BEAT INTERNET TROLLS

 < 300 Seconds

[A] troll is someone who posts inflammatory, extraneous, or off-topic messages in an online community with the primary intent of provoking other users into a desired emotional response . . .

—*Wikipedia ('Troll')*

Chat rooms, Facebook, Twitter, YouTube, online games, discussion forums and almost everywhere else you look on the Internet, you are sure to find trolls—who are incessantly trying to tempt people to respond to illogical, pointless and insensitive remarks. Recognize them from your favourite websites? Trolls get a kick out of insulting the victim and spoiling their mood, online experience or even their reputation. Most trolls use poor grammar, throw insults around, attack you for no real reason and will often type in all caps. They might even post the same message in multiple websites and forums, to get reactions from as many people as possible. So how do you deal with a troll?

Unfortunately, we don't yet have a program or app that can make your Internet experience completely troll-free. So the first rule of dealing with a troll is, no matter how hurt, angry or sad the troll has made you, never express your frustration and anger directly to them. Do not ever engage in a verbal fight or sarcastic battle with the troll. Replying to a troll with facts, figures and logical arguments is also not always the best idea, since trolls will always find a way to misquote you or find more fodder within your factually accurate answer to troll you with. The secret to remember is that the troll will be interested in continuing to play with you only if they realize that it's affecting you, or if you give them attention.

Instead, reply to a troll by keeping calm, writing a controlled and matter-of-fact response, keeping emotions at bay, and trying firmly to bring the discussion back to the topic. Chances are that this will frustrate the troll and encourage them to move to more volatile targets. Sometimes, even posting a mild compliment might surprise and silence the troll. If nothing works, the most effective way to deal with a troll is to simply ignore them.

Does that mean that you will never face an attack from trolls again? Be prepared, for you always will. Trolls will always be there on the Internet, so you just have to learn how to live with them. Of course, if everything else fails, you can always block a troll.

95. HOW TO STAY INSPIRED IN LIFE

 < 180 Seconds

Most of us are so busy with our daily routines that we tend to forget what is really important to us—our big-picture life goals. Wouldn't it be great if there was an app that kept reminding, inspiring and motivating us to take steps towards achieving what is really important to us, so that we could remain happy, focused and productive?

Bloom is an iOS app that can be downloaded free of cost from the iTunes app store or from the **https://www.mindbloom.com/bloom** website. It is an app that brings inspiration to your mobile phone in a visually awe-inspiring way. It allows you to combine your goals with powerful photos and your favourite music to create inspiring reminders of what is really important to you—eating healthy, spending more time with your family, remembering to call your grandma, driving safely, getting pumped up before a workout, cheering up in the middle of the bad day at work, drinking plenty of water to stay healthy, taking the stairs instead of the escalator and others.

Bloom and the Bloom logo are registered trademarks of Mindbloom Inc., used with permission.

When you initially start the **Bloom** app, a few default inspirational ideas (also known as **Blooms**) will be displayed on the screen, to get you comfortable with the app. To create your own **Bloom**, press **Add** > **Create a Bloom**. Enter any inspirational text you want. In this example, I am going to create a health-related Bloom—'work out for 45 mins'. Press **Next** to continue.

Bloom and the Bloom logo are registered trademarks of Mindbloom Inc., used with permission.

Choose a suitable image that goes well with your inspirational message. You can either take a new photo using your camera, or choose one from the collection of photos available within **Bloom**.

Bloom and the Bloom logo are registered trademarks of Mindbloom Inc., used with permission.

You can also add background music to your **Bloom**. The idea here is that the inspiring text, image and background music will all work together to motivate you to on your life goals. Instead of using just one image and one text in a **Bloom**, it is possible to use several images and multiple texts to create a **Bloom** video as well. Your **Bloom** is now ready to inspire you to achieve one of your life goals.

You can schedule your **Blooms** to be automatically displayed on your screen at predefined specific dates and times, or at completely random dates and times! Just select the **Bloom** you want to schedule reminders for, press the **Edit** button > Go to **Remind Me**.

Bloom and the Bloom logo are registered trademarks of Mindbloom Inc., used with permission.

Bloom and the Bloom logo are registered trademarks of Mindbloom Inc., used with permission.

If you want to share your **Blooms** with your friends, or if you have **Blooms** that are applicable to your family members or your entire team at office, you can choose to share them via email or social networking websites.

With the **Bloom** app on your mobile device, you will never be too far from the next dose of your inspiration!

96. HOW TO SEND FREE SMS TEXT MESSAGES FROM YOUR GMAIL ACCOUNT

 < 120 Seconds

Google has recently introduced a free SMS-to-mobile-phones service for Gmail users. This feature allows users to send and receive SMS text messages to and from mobile phone devices. To enable the SMS feature in your Gmail account, click on **Settings > Labs > Scroll** down to the **SMS in Chat** feature and select **Enable**, and then scroll down to click on **Save Changes**.

SMS in Chat and the SMS in Chat logo are registered trademarks of Google Inc., used with permission.

SMS in Chat and the SMS in Chat logo are registered trademarks of Google Inc., used with permission.

Now you can start sending text messages from your Gmail account to anyone in your contact list. Simply click on the contact's name in the chat app to the left of your Gmail window. In the pop-up chat window, click on **More > Send Text (SMS)** option.

It will now ask you to enter the mobile phone number that you want to associate with the selected Gmail contact. Type the number in the space provided and click on the **Save** button. Most countries in the world are already supported by the Gmail SMS feature.

SMS in Chat and the SMS in Chat logo are registered trademarks of Google Inc., used with permission.

SMS in Chat and the SMS in Chat logo are registered trademarks of Google Inc., used with permission.

You are now ready to start sending SMS text messages to your contact. Simply type the SMS text message in the space provided—just the way you would type a regular chat message—and press enter to send the SMS text message to your contact.

The Gmail SMS feature is free, but it is restricted by a system of credits. If you look carefully at the chat window, you will find that Gmail displays the number of SMS credits that you have left in your account. By default, when you enable the SMS feature in your Gmail account, you are given fifty SMS credits free of charge. Each time you send an SMS text message, your available credits are decreased by one. However, each time someone replies to you by sending an SMS text message to your Gmail account, your SMS credits are increased by five.

Using this feature, you can use Gmail to send an SMS text message to your own phone, and then reply to that text message as many times you want. Each time you respond, your SMS credits will be increased by five, up to a maximum limit of fifty SMS credits. Moreover, in case your SMS credits go down to zero, all you need to do is wait until the next day, and automatically your SMS credit will be increased by one.

97. HOW TO GET A FAKE INCOMING CALL TO GET OUT OF STICKY SITUATIONS

 < 60 Seconds

Fake-A-Call and the Fake-A-Call logo are registered trademarks of ExcellTech Inc., used with permission.

Have you ever got stuck talking to a boring colleague, boss, date or relative and wished that there was an excuse to get you out of there? Wouldn't it be great if your best friend called you at that very moment and pretended to be in an emergency situation that required your immediate attention?

Fake-A-Call is a fake-call app available for both iOS and Android phones. Once installed on your phone, you can choose the caller name, caller photo, ringtone and even when you wish to receive the call. If you don't want to bother entering these details, you can simply pick someone from your contacts list.

98. HOW TO USE A FAKE SMS TO GET OUT OF TROUBLE

 < 60 Seconds

Have you ever been in a situation where you were in trouble and no one believed the excuses you cooked up? Wouldn't it be great if you were able to show an actual SMS text message on your mobile phone as proof supporting your excuse? For example, you may have used an urgent doctor's appointment as an excuse for showing up late at an important client meeting, and want to show a text message from the doctor as proof. This is now possible with the **Fake SMS & Call** app.

Fake SMS & Call and the Fake SMS & Call logo are registered trademarks of Fake SMS & Call, used with permission.

Download and launch **Fake SMS & Call** on your phone and enter all the details of the fake SMS text message you want, including the sender's number, time, date and the actual message. You can even choose whether you want the fake SMS message to appear as a received message or a sent message. Once you have entered all the relevant details, simply press the **Create Message** button.

If you now go to the inbox on your

Fake SMS & Call and the Fake SMS & Call logo are registered trademarks of Fake SMS & Call.

Fake SMS & Call and the Fake SMS & Call logo are registered trademarks of Fake SMS & Call.

mobile phone, you will be able to see the fake SMS message in it. It is important to note that this app does not actually send or receive any message, it merely places a fake message on your phone based on the details that you entered in the previous step. The best part is that if you were to show the SMS text message to someone else, there is no way for them to tell whether the message is real or fake. You can also reply to a fake message with a real message if you wanted to.

To make your story even more believable, **Fake SMS & Call** also allows you add fake entries to the call logs of your mobile phone. Simply tap the **Call** tab on the top right corner of the app and enter all the details of the fake call you wish to add to the call logs of your mobile phone.

If you were to view the call logs on your mobile phone, you will now be able to view the fake call with all the details that you entered in the previous step.

99. HOW TO SEND AND RECEIVE TEXT MESSAGES FROM YOUR ANDROID PHONE USING YOUR COMPUTER

 < 120 Seconds

Imagine that you are sitting in a meeting with your boss and colleagues, and you receive a text message on your mobile phone from a friend. Although you are itching to pick up your phone, read the message and reply to it, you cannot do that since it might be construed as rude. Or, maybe you have forgotten your mobile phone at home and still wanted to text your friends while you are sitting in the office.

MightyText is an Android-based app that allows you to remotely control and access all the text messaging features on your phone through the Internet from any computer or tablet in any part of the world. While your boss or colleagues will think that you are dilligently typing notes into your computer, in reality you will be texting!

To use this feature, first download the **MightyText** app on your Android phone. It is available as a free download from the Google Play App Store. When you run **MightyText** for the first time on your Android phone, press the **Complete Setup** button to link the app with your Google account. This is required so that you can verify your identity whenever you want to read and reply to your text messages from a computer or tablet.

Once you have installed **MightyText**, you can use any computer or tablet to connect to the web interface of the app at **https://mightytext.net/app**. You will be asked to log in to the same Google account that you had used while setting up the app on your Android phone. Once you log in, you will be able to control all the text messaging functions on your mobile phone remotely through the Internet, including:

1. Read and reply to all the text messages on your Android phone remotely from your computer or tablet
2. Receive new text messages, which will immediately show up on your browser as soon as they appear on your Android phone; you can even reply to them right there from within your browser
3. Search, read and reply to all your old messages
4. Compose new text messages to start new conversations with your friends

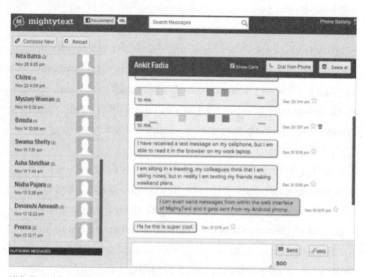

MightyText and the MightyText logo are registered trademarks of MightyText, used with permission.

Another benefit of using **MightyText** is that it saves time, since most people can type messages faster on their computer than on their mobile phone. **MightyText** can be used in the same way on your tablet as you used it on your computer.

MightyText also instantly displays alerts on your computer to inform you about incoming calls that you may have received or missed on your Android phone.

MightyText and the MightyText logo are registered trademarks of MightyText, used with permission.

Finally, you can also use **MightyText** to make phone calls from your Android phone. However, the big limitation of this feature is that you can only initiate a phone call from your computer. You will still need to physically pick up your Android phone to continue the conversation.

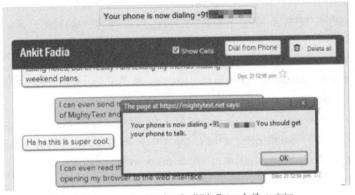

MightyText and the MightyText logo are registered trademarks of MightyText, used with permission.

Also, please remember that even though you are using the Internet to control messaging functions on your phone, standard messaging and calling rates will be applicable on all usage of **MightyText**.

100. HOW TO WIRELESSLY TRANSFER FILES FROM PHONE TO PHONE

 < 120 Seconds

Wouldn't it be great if there was a way to share stuff with your friends by simply shaking hands with them? Science fiction, you say? It is actually possible—well, almost. An easy, fast and almost magical way to wirelessly transfer files between any two devices (mobile phones, tablets or computers) is to use an app called **Bump**.

Bump is available as a free download from **https://bu.mp** and can be run on Android and iOS phones, or even through the Internet connection on your computer. **Bump** allows you to wirelessly transfer files between any two devices by simply doing a gentle fist bump between the two devices. For example, imagine you are at a conference and want to exchange contact information with someone that you just met. You can wirelessly exchange the details by simply doing a fist bump with them! Think of **Bump** as a modern-day equivalent of a handshake with a business contact, which automatically allows you to exchange business cards with each other.

Whenever you bump two devices, the **Bump** app running on each of the devices will record their respective GPS coordinates and transmit them to the central **Bump** server. The sensors on the two devices will also literally 'feel the bump' and transmit the **Bump Details** to the central **Bump** server. The central **Bump** server

Bump and the Bump logo are registered trademarks of Bump Technologies Inc., used with permission.

will use the GPS coordinates and **Bump Details** to match up the two devices and establish a data communication channel between them. When you send **Bump** files to your friend's device, the files are getting transmitted using Internet connections on both the devices.

For example, imagine a situation where I have taken some holiday photos with my mobile phone, and want to **Bump** them to my friend John Doe. For that to happen, both John and I need to start the **Bump** app on our phones. Once **Bump** is launched, I have to select all the photos I want to share with John.

Now, while holding our mobile phones in our hands in the normal position, John and I have to do a gentle fist bump. Immediately, the **Bump** app kicks in and displays a notification on the screens of both the mobile phones that the other person is trying to establish a connection. For the selected photos to be exchanged between the two phones, both John and I need to press the **Connect** button.

Bump and the Bump logo are registered trademarks of Bump Technologies Inc., used with permission.

Bump and the Bump logo are registered trademarks of Bump Technologies Inc., used with permission.

Within a few seconds, the selected photos will be transferred from my phone to John's phone via **Bump**. Similarly, it is also possible to use **Bump** to exchange business cards with someone else by simply doing a gentle fist bump with them.

Once you are back from a long holiday, you can use **Bump** to even transfer photos from your phone to your laptop. Start your browser and connect to **https://bu.mp**. Open **Bump** on your mobile phone and select the photos you wish to bump to your laptop. Connect your phone to your laptop by pressing the spacebar key with your mobile phone. A connection notification will now be displayed on both your mobile phone and your browser screens. Press the **Connect** button on your mobile phone to transfer the selected photos.

Soon enough, the selected photos will be magically transferred from your mobile phone to your desktop and displayed in your browser. No need for wires or anything! **Bump** will allow you to either save the photos on your computer or instantly share them with your friends.